FUTURE
GOALS

GENEVIVE CHAMBLEE

HOT TREE PUBLISHING

Locker Room Love

FUTURE GOALS

LOCKER ROOM LOVE
BOOK 5

GENEVIVE CHAMBLEE

HOT TREE PUBLISHING

For information, contact the publisher, Hot Tree Publishing.

WWW.HOTTREEPUBLISHING.COM

EDITING: HOT TREE EDITING

COVER DESIGNER: BOOKSMITH DESIGN

E-BOOK ISBN: 978-1-922359-81-0

PAPERBACK ISBN: 978-1-922359-82-7

This book is not dedicated to any petty, rude, trifling, or spiteful people. Instead, it is dedicated to decent folks, aka the rest of humankind. Life is a playground. Enjoy it while you can. Stereotypes are not genuine definitions, and everything is possible.

To CKMC, I would like to say that it's true. Mommy knows best.

Finally, to my precious Leah. You are so missed.

FOREWORD

Although *Future Goals* is part of the *Locker Room Love* series, it can be read as a standalone novel. However, readers should be aware that there are some plot points and/or storylines that overarch across all books in the series. As a result, not all plot points or storylines in *Future Goals* may have a finite resolution at this time.

Additionally, this story is about breaking down barriers and busting stereotypes. It may tackle topics that are difficult to discuss.

The story is set in South Louisiana. Some of the terms, phrases, and sentence structures used are common regional expressions and may at first glance seem like a typo or grammatical error. For example, "What did you say?" may be expressed as "What you said?" "Why do you care?" may be expressed as "What care you?" Instead of "buying groceries" or "putting up groceries," it is common to say "making groceries" or "saving groceries" or "make a bill." There may be times when verbs are intentionally omitted. For example, the question "Who is that?" is famously expressed as "Who dat?" Furthermore, characters may speak using proper grammar in a professional setting but revert to their regional dialect when relaxed or in informal environments.

TEAM ROSTERS

Lafayette Ice Water Moccasins
(Minor League)
Dalek "Taz" Tazandlakova
Ian Whittaker
Kaden Blanc
Eric Chapel
Donavan Sawyer
Stavos Pokrefrke
Sartor Tzotzolas
Dustin Ames
Chandler
Pernell (coach)

Rebels
(Minor League)
Oliver Nash
Wayne
Barlow
Peters
Rich
Hyatt
Kitchens
Kelly

Wolves
Beau Doucet
Brody Simmons
Thad Clark
Gagon
Pittman

Owls
Timothée Croneau (former)
Aidan Lefèvre (former)
Giles Wayne
Nowak

Northcove Mutineers
Timothée Croneau
Benoit
Walsh
Andrew Calhern
Gerrick Polak
Pierre Tremblay
Joe Hales
Carter (trainer)
Bert Addison (coach)

Saint Anne Civets
Christophe Fortenot
Aidan Lefèvre
Gatien Glesseau
Brighton Rabalais
Semien Metoyèr
Nicco Bale
Vadium Stepanov
Francis Gillory
Jasper Jordan
Ludvig Enok
Rory Cathey (coach)
Carlton Varner (general manger)
Michael Darbonne (owner)
Harold Whittle (owner)
Shaw (owner)

ULSA Minotaurs (College)
Corrigan Ellery
Bowen "Bo" Nguyen
Ramsey "Rams" Theriot
Shade Franley
Roland Cardenas
Shelby Kavanaugh
Thad Hansford
Reid Larousse
Miles Posey
Hen Sweeten
Marshall Girid
Owen Massey (Coach)
Paul DeSevren (Asst. Coach)

1

CORRIGAN

Tick, tick, tick.

"Which way is it?" Corrigan wondered aloud, turning his smartphone to rotate the digital campus map and hoping something would look remotely familiar, or at least less Southern plantation. Rows of antebellum buildings—the very definition of grandeur and prestige—situated on tidy squares of impeccably manicured lawns adorned with hydrangeas, azaleas, and camellias surrounded him. Pretty for a tourist. Not so much for someone with a scheduled practice. When he'd toured the campus three months ago, it hadn't seemed as overwhelming or daunting. Then again, perhaps having a personal tour guide and being chauffeured in a snazzy Cushman Hauler had cast an illusion of simplicity.

He'd caught himself paying attention to the names boldly etched across the fronts of buildings, but it did little to help him presently.

The tree-killer map he held in his other hand listed the buildings by numbers, and the legend arranged them in alphabetical and not numerical order. And with all the construction, the phone's GPS Walking Directions feature kept steering him to a labyrinth of tall scaffolding, orange barricades, chain-link fences encircling heavy equipment, and impassible stacks of steel girders. The results: he was lost as fuck.

Dammit, he wasn't aspiring to rival or reincarnate Lewis and fucking Clark in expedition. The world had been mapped, and as far as he knew, it wasn't flat. But it sure as hell felt as if he was about to fall off the face of the Earth. Okay, perhaps that was a tad of an exaggeration. He only needed to get to Prograis Athletic Centre, the PAC for short, which a reasonable person would assume to be located near the athletic dorms. But no! Of course not. Not on this campus. Just like the financial aid office didn't grace the same hemisphere as the registrar's office, and the office for student affairs didn't issue student identification cards. To add to the crap pile, he'd been bumped from his flight due to over-booking. Because fuck his life!

His stomach lurched at the thought of being late. The coach had been clear. Tardiness would not be tolerated unless a limb was being amputated, and even in that instance, it depended on which limb and the credentials of the surgeon.

I can do this, he told himself with little certitude as he arbitrarily chose a direction. More precisely, he *had* to do it. As cliché as it sounded—and oh, how he detested being cliché, not that he ever was—he had no turning back option. Well... he could, but the consequences of doing so would suck, and he'd had enough suckage in his life. How would he look his parents in the eye when they had been so proud? Eh, maybe not so much *proud* as relieved, and perhaps even relieved was too strong of a word. Maybe it should be called laissez-faire, as said in this region, with a splash of reduced burden. Not that his parents would call him that to his face—at least, not these days. They wouldn't, not because it wasn't true, but because his father couldn't remember, and his mother lacked the energy to recall.

I really can, he continued convincing himself, something he'd been doing all morning. He belonged here. He'd worked for it. He'd earned it. For years, he'd sweated and trained despite the badgering and disparagement from peers, friends, and relatives who only visited on holidays. Even many of his teachers—the very people expected to support and encourage betterment—had joined the naysaying group. However, that was the past, and at present, he had no time for reflection. He was smack-dab in the middle of his own not-so-remarkable White Rabbit moment—minus the waistcoat and gloves—and getting upset wasn't going to improve the situation.

You got into college. Use your head. Technically, sports and not brains had gotten him into college, but he wouldn't argue semantics with himself at the moment. He was here now. Besides, a shortage of smarts had not been the reason for his dismal academic performance. Other circumstances attributed to his academic challenges. But his coach wouldn't give a shit about circumstances if Corrigan didn't haul his ass into practice on time. Bottom line. Fact.

He tilted his chin up defiantly toward the sky, recalling the one day of Youth Brigade Camp, a Boy Scouts of America knockoff group, he'd attended in grammar school before it was disbanded for low interest. "The sun rises east and sets west." It wasn't a groundbreaking revelation, but it gave Corrigan a starting point. Although the buildings blocked much of the sky, the small piece that peeked between the trees appeared brighter to his left. According to the map, his destination was located on the east side of campus. Maybe.

With nothing to lose, he turned left at the large octagonal building that seemed out of place among the rest. He rotated his map again as he rounded the building. *Finally!*

As the stadium came into sight, he suppressed the excitement of relief in case it was a mirage or angst-conjured hallucination. Two years ago at camp, he'd been tricked into consuming pizza with shrooms sprinkled atop. His so-called teammates thought it would be hilarious to witness him scampering through the dorm hallways with his jockstrap perched on his head. Fortunately, he'd experienced minimal effects and disappointed his teammates, but he'd heard habitual users claim that flashbacks could occur years later. Could now be it? He had no time to ponder the thought. He still wasn't where he needed to be, but the stadium was within view. If his memory served correctly, two miles on the other side of the stadium sat the arena.

Picking up the pace, he hurried across a parking lot and down a steep hill that he would bet his last dollar wasn't meant for foot traffic. Well, lawn maintenance would have to get over it, because there was absolutely no way he'd be on time following the sidewalk. However, cutting through the stadium would shave off at minimum a half mile. As luck would have it—and he could stand a bit of luck at the moment—one of the stadium gates was open for workers hauling in buckets of paint, industrial cleaner, and new chairbacks. No one noticed—or if they did, no one cared, which was more likely the case—as Corrigan slipped inside the ninety-thousand-seater.

Swiping the sweat from his forehead with his arm, he eyed crew workers meticulously painting the Astroturf as he trudged across Robichaux Field. He got it. Football was the omnipotent sport of gods. Nothing reigned more supreme in the South, and every aspect of the university was arranged for the utmost convenience of the pigskin Olympians of Beauvais Hall. But could the hockey arena have been situated any farther off the main campus? Another foot and it would plunge into the abyss of Minotaur athletics.

He supposed he shouldn't complain. The exercise would help loosen his muscles for practice. But damn if his weighty backpack didn't feel as if it gained five pounds with each step like a waterlogged boot camp torture exercise. Who gave homework and reading assignments before the first day of classes? Yet, honestly, the mound of newly purchased textbooks wasn't the problem—although, he much would have appreciated an e-book option. No, the humidity was the culprit threatening to drag him to his knees. How did people breathe in such heat? The Bronx got hot but nothing close to this Louisiana stratosphere of suffocation and misery. He willed himself not to think about it.

As he reached the end zone, it dawned on him that he hadn't considered if a second gate would be open for him to exit. If not, he'd be royally screwed. It was fair to say strategic planning wasn't his strongest suit, but if he intended on completing college, it was a skill he needed improving.

Fortunately, he had his pick of outlets as a flurry of workers scurried to unload crates from two eighteen-wheelers in preparation for the season opener in three weeks. *What it must feel like to have ninety thousand screaming fans.*

He continued onward, exiting to a flat concrete path leading to a bell tower. *Hot damn!* The tower he remembered from his orientation tour. He was certain he was headed in the right direction now.

After eight additional minutes of jogging—

huffing and puffing at this point—the PAC appeared ahead of him, and the air seemed to sweeten. In two additional minutes, he found himself on the front steps. A burst of cool air hit him the second he pulled open the tinted glass door. *Ahh, heaven.* However, as welcomed as escaping the unrelenting July sun was, he had no time to relish it. He still needed to find the locker room.

Rounding a corner, Corrigan nearly smashed into a wall of chest adorned in an ULSA T-shirt, a shiny whistle dangling on a lanyard, and a badge.

Shit! Coach.

Assistant Coach Paul DeSevren folded his muscle-swollen arms. "You're late," he snapped, his gruff voice oozing with irritation.

"Sorry, Coach. I got lost. It won't happen again."

"It better not." DeSevren's gaze scanned Corrigan slowly from head to toe, and his expression relaxed a notch. "Did you walk here from the dorm?"

Corrigan nodded. "Yes, sir."

"May I ask why you didn't take the shuttle?"

Shuttle? There's a shuttle?

Corrigan's expression must have given the coach his answer, because he shook his head before Corrigan could respond. "I've been telling Owen those campus tours are shit." Making a tsking noise, he scribbled something on his clipboard and then jerked his head toward the corridor on his left. "Hurry it up. Everyone else has signed in."

That's it? Corrigan's entire body practically jittered with relief. This was his hall pass, likely the only one he'd ever receive, and he wouldn't take it for granted. As expressed in the antiquated idiom dictated by a thousand old wives, never stare a gift horse in the mouth even if it's wearing wooden dentures—or something to that nature. All he knew was he was appreciative of the assistant coach not chewing him out.

"Yes, sir," Corrigan responded, thankful for the reprieve.

His gaze floated to the numerous framed professional jerseys of former ULSA players who had advanced to the professional league, the most recent two being Semien Metoyèr and Brighton Rabalais, both playing for the Saint Anne Civets. One day, Corrigan's professional jersey could be hanging there beside them. True, less than 2 percent of college players made pro, but it could happen. So when the NHL trumpet sounded its recruiting call, Corrigan would have to make sure he got in that number. The thought played in his head to the tune of "When the Saints Go Marching In," indicating that Louisiana was already beginning to rub off on the part of him that hadn't sweated onto the pavement.

"Go on. Git!" DeSevren ordered, snapping Corrigan from his fantasy.

"Right."

Music overlayed with chanting, laughing, and clapping drifted from down the corridor, and a charge rippled through his bloodstream and warmed his skin. A new realization swept over him. For months, he'd been waiting for this moment, and now it was about to happen. His gut churned with nervous excitement, and the anticipation of meeting his new teammates for the first time—his brethren for the next four years—distorted his face with a goofy expression, resembling a person straining to hold in flatulence. Or… maybe it wasn't anxiety he felt.

Holy mother of shit! That bowl of porridge with apples and raisins, sourdough biscuit, and skinny latte probably wasn't the best breakfast option. His stomach rumbled again, and he inwardly grimaced. *Planning.* He must do better.

Blowing out a shaky breath, he followed the clamor down the corridor. With each step, his heart thumped hard and quick, then stilled once he reached the locker room door. Above the head, a bronzed inscribed hockey stick read *"Les rêves deviennent réalité un changement à la fois."* Corrigan didn't speak French, but he'd seen the team motto written enough times to know it translated to "Dreams come true one shift at a time." Yes, he was about to step into his dream, which would make it a reality. All the exasperation from earlier dwindled as the elation of this moment preempted everything else. When he opened the door, the applauding, whistling, and cheering crescendoed.

"Percolator," someone yelled.

A few seconds later, someone called, "Charlie Brown."

Half-dressed men gathered in a circle cheered and recorded on their cell phones as several men in the center appeared to be having an old-school dance-off.

"The Carlton," another player who looked every inch of a young Billy Idol but with freckles and braces announced.

A guy with bulky arms resembling Popeye the Sailor Man pointed at him. "Dude, if I throw my back out doing this crazy shit, I'm going to kick your ass."

A burst of laughter erupted from the group but

immediately began fading at the sound of the door closing behind Corrigan. As more team members stared in his direction, voices quieted and smiles ebbed. Lips pressed in taut lines and curled downward as faces scrunched as if odors of rotting vermin and waste in the sewers had seeped through the facility's vents. The music abruptly stopped, and the room filled with a deafening silence. Corrigan suppressed a shudder at the iciness that now consumed the space. Suddenly, the room felt much smaller.

"You lost, jungle monkey?" Bulky Arms snarled.

A flurry of emotions raced through Corrigan, and he balled his fists at his side, yet the shock robbed him of his speech. Pooling tears stung the backs of his charcoal-colored eyes, but he blinked them away, avoiding providing evidence of his humiliation and pain as his absurd unbridled optimism plunged into a black hole. Only by the grace of God did his feet remain in place, preventing his fist from streaking into Bulky Arms' condescending mug and dragging him over the river and through the woods to Grandma's house.

A player who appeared to be of Asian descent shoved the guy in the arm. "Hey, man, not cool."

"Clamp it, Nguyen," Bulky Arms hissed.

"Um… the basketball pavilion is next door," a tall redhead with his hair twisted in a man bun added, his voice laced with a mixture of empathy and bewilderment.

Corrigan's muscles coiled tighter.

"When I call a practice," a deep voice boomed from the opposite side of the room, "at 10:00 a.m., that does not mean 10:01 a.m. or 10:06 a.m., or whatever hell time you decide to show up, Ellery. This is not a garden party where your presence is optional or a red-carpet event for you to make a dramatic entrance in a stunning ensemble. You will be on time or not bother being on this team. Do I make myself clear?"

Corrigan turned, along with the rest of the team, to face Head Coach Owen Massey at the end of the long row of benches.

"Yes, sir," Corrigan replied, responding to his surname.

"As for the rest of you," Coach Massey continued, "you should already be warmed up on the ice and not in here waving your pricks around and acting like a group of prepubescent clowns." He cast a warning glare at Bulky Arms. "Theriot, as captain, I expect you to make sure each member of this team is where he is supposed to be when he is supposed to be there. You are *all* your brothers' keeper."

Captain? Corrigan's frown deepened. This asswipe was Ramsey Theriot, the center he'd heard nothing but how amazing and upstanding of a player he was?

Nodding, Theriot replied with the assertiveness of a military private. "Sure thing, Coach."

"Now, everyone, dress out and be on the ice in three minutes," he commanded, turning to leave. "Not four. Not three and a half. Three."

There was a collective "Yes, Coach," as players scrambled to tug on jerseys, pads, and skates.

Theriot peered over his shoulder at Corrigan with a blunted countenance, but an edge remained in his voice. "Freshmen stalls are by the toilets."

Welcome to ULSA.

2

SACHA

So, this is what being banished feels like, Sacha wondered as he stood on the steps of Weymouth Law Center and overlooked the ULSA campus. One fuckup and no redemption. Weymouths weren't supposed to lose.

Thirty years. Wow! He ran his fingers through his sun-streaked auburn hair. He still couldn't fathom that his client had gotten thirty years. Honestly, he'd feel worse had his client been innocent, but for defense attorneys, innocence was an optional luxury. Losing the case maimed his ego, but the sentence had sealed his fate to academia hell and decimated his career trajectory goals. He should be in a courtroom and not some damn classroom as a teacher's assistant babysitting pre-adults. Hell, he hadn't liked school when he'd been *in* school. However, this was what happened with failure at his firm… with his family. They might as well condemn him to the guillotine or airdrop him into Siberia with three days' rations and no shoes.

He slumped against a cast stone column, his sleek tailored suit easily differentiating him from the main student body despite his baby face, and sighed. It wasn't his fault his client lied on the stand. *Pshaw*, his client had lied to him—repeatedly. And convincingly. Over and over, his client had insisted there were no foreign bank accounts. Sacha had even had his people—some of the best in the business—investigate to validate the existence of no such accounts, and they'd come up with zilch. But the prosecution had managed to find not one. Not two. Not even three. But *four* accounts. Four fucking offshore accounts with hundreds of thousands in each. And why had they found them? Because despite Sacha warning his client not to talk to anyone, his client couldn't keep his trap shut—or dick soft—and ended up drunk blabbering to an undercover agent in a micromini and with blow-up tits. His intoxicated ramblings relayed enough details that the prosecution had been able to hunt down all they needed at the eleventh hour.

But even the discovery of this incriminating information hadn't been enough to bake their uncooked chicken. No, it had been the lying. Since Sacha's client had been caught perjuring himself during cross-examination, the judge allowed the prosecution to bring it all in as evidence—evidence that Sacha previously, and masterfully, if he said so himself, had gotten suppressed. Talk about an epic clusterfuck. In eight short minutes, the entire case he'd built for weeks before the jury had been decimated to shit. All that effort for what? Nothing. Absolutely nothing. *Beep, beep, bitch! Off to jail you go.*

"Hey," Paxton called, exiting the frosty glass doors. "What are you doing?"

Sacha sighed again. "Nothing. Just needed some air."

Paxton's molten silver eyes softened knowingly at his younger sibling. "It's going to be okay. It's not half as bad as you think."

"Don't serve me that bucket of fish heads. This is your jam. You're here by choice and can still practice."

"You can still practice, geez. No one stripped you of your license."

Sacha's pained expression didn't change.

"Think of it as a refresher, a getting back to basics."

Uh-huh. Being a lackey. "Maybe I should join a monastery. Leave Saint Anne altogether." If he wasn't in a courtroom, what was the point of even having a law degree? Trials were his power source—his big bang and sonic boom all rolled into one.

"Now you're talking gibberish. You haven't even given this a chance. You're assuming instead of basing your summation on facts."

This elicited a weak smile from Sacha. "Clever."

"Here, why don't you take this over to the PAC?" Paxton shoved a large, overstuffed manila envelope toward Sacha.

"What is it?"

"Some contracts that need to get signed. The names and instructions are on the top."

So, the gophering starts now. Sacha screwed up his face.

"I know it's nothing exciting or revolutionary that will have you marching the stairs of the Supreme Court, but it'll get you away from here for a while, and you seem like you could use the break."

True. As far away from this place—the constant reminder of his failure—he could get, the better. Each time he crossed the threshold, he felt a piece of his soul rip out of his body. But if he was ever to regain his position, he would have to claw his way back up the corporate ladder, starting at the bottom rung and playing the game as the rules had been set.

"Fine." He accepted the envelope.

"Good." Paxton smiled.

Sacha returned the smile with less enthusiasm. Despite being six years younger, he and Paxton could pass for twins with the same lean build, plump lips, deep-set eyes, Nordic nose, and square jaw. But the similarities stopped there. Personality-wise, they were opposites, with Sacha being what his friends referred to as careful and tight-assed and Paxton as dynamic and cavalier.

"Now that's settled, why don't you come over tonight for supper? The kids are at camp, and Gretchen would love to see you."

Sacha inwardly cringed—not that he didn't like his sister-in-law. On the contrary, he thought the world of her, not to mention her cooking, being a chef and all. He wasn't one to turn down a free meal. However, he always felt out of place, like a third wheel, around the two of them. Their love radiated off each other like some cosmic event. Sacha had never experienced anything close to what the two of them seemed to have, and, at times, he doubted he ever would. For as much as he dated, he never became enthused by the women he found himself meeting. They were always *meh*. And knowing his brother the way he did, this wasn't a random invitation for a tasty meal. Sacha could smell another setup a mile away. No surprise there. It had been months since Paxton last arranged him a blind date. Sacha presumed it was Paxton's turn in the family who-fixes-Sacha-up roulette. A few weeks ago, it had been his sister and the prior month his mother. He probably held the record for the most dead-end setups. What was worse was that he wasn't even getting his dick wet. He'd all but resolved himself to being in an exclusive relationship with his right hand. Well, truthfully, he was ambidextrous, and if he got creative and contorted himself in the correct position, he could use his—

He interrupted his self-deprecating thought before it could go any further.

"I'm sure your wife would prefer to spend the evening alone with her husband."

"We spend plenty of time together."

"Uh-huh. Who is she?"

Paxton grinned. "One of the sous-chefs at the new restaurant."

Sacha groaned. "Pax, we've talked about this."

"It's one meal, not a blood sacrifice. It won't kill you." He looked in the opposite direction and lowered his voice. "And it's not like you have plans or anything."

"Right, because my life is so pathetic." Which wasn't far from the truth if Sacha was counting all the things going right in his life at the moment. "Thanks for reminding me."

"That's not what I meant."

"Sure it isn't." Shoving one hand in his pocket, he started down the steps. "Why do you do this to me?"

"Because you are entitled to and shall receive the same bullshit the rest of us must. I didn't get a memo saying you were exempt."

"What time?"

"Six."

Oh, goodie. Plenty of time to fill the day with suckage. Beginning with occupying his afternoon meeting with a gaggle—well, nearly a gaggle—of banal, pompous, unappreciative, obtuse jocks.

3

CORRIGAN

THE SOUND OF THE VULCANIZED RUBBER SMACKING against the ice followed by the thwack of it against a stick resumed after a brief recess that had lasted long enough for Coach Massey to reorder the line... again... and bark out new instructions... again. The play called for the center, Theriot, to pass the puck to the right-winger. Simple enough—or so Corrigan would have thought.

Everything went south from the start when Corrigan lost his footing at the drop. Call him peculiar, but the ice felt different from that at his old rink, and he hadn't adjusted. Yet his tripping hadn't been what mucked up the sequence. Shelby Kavanaugh pitchforked the puck to center ice, and

Miles Posey picked it up. Posey turned at the line with Hen Sweeten in front. Corrigan attempted to get past Sweeten, but Shade Franley, defenseman for the opposing line, closed him off. Swooping in, Theriot stole the puck from Posey. However, after looking to his left and spotting Corrigan as his left-winger and clearly the open man and sensible choice, Theriot passed right, overshooting his unexpected right-winger, Roland Cardenas, and sending it onto the stick of Franley. Nothing about this sequence had been executed well.

Conceivably, Corrigan could rationalize—to make himself feel more accepted and convince himself that Theriot was less of a jerk—that the captain had made his choice due to his left side weakness. The assessment wouldn't have been completely inaccurate. Most left-handed shooters— and Theriot fell into that category—favored passing to the right due to their dominant hand being positioned at the top of their stick. If the theory held true with Theriot, then what happened on the ice wasn't personal but rather Theriot covering a handicap or, at the very least, reacting instinctually.

Yes, Corrigan *could* think that. But he wouldn't. Why should he make excuses for someone else's shitty behavior? He may not be able to present irrefutable proof, but he sensed why Theriot had neglected to pass the puck to him. What he couldn't do was blame his shock on the captain. This was hockey. This was the South. It was something Corrigan probably should have expected—not because he deserved it but because it wasn't something unusual. He'd heard a lot. Read a lot in history books. Watched plenty of documentaries. The element of surprise should have been removed from the table.

A high-pitched shrill of a whistle pierced and echoed throughout the rink.

"Is this what we're doing?" Coach Massey shouted. "Everyone designing their own plays now like Tennessee Williams? Or were you expecting some Georges Méliès special effects to make that wreckage work? Or maybe we're in the Land of Make Believe, and a miniature trolly's about to pop around the corner and transport us all to a magic castle with unicorns and hockey goals that jump in front of pucks. Explain to me what was going on out there."

"Ellery wasn't in position," Theriot blurted. "He's too slow to keep up."

Asshole!

Although Corrigan wanted to protest that he

had been in position, the second half of Theriot's statement had been true, at least partially. Corrigan had kept up with his teammates but just barely. Until two years ago, he'd played defense. Then he'd caught mononucleosis—from where or whom remained a mystery. As a result, he'd lost twenty-two pounds, and he'd struggled to regain any of it. His former coach declared him too small at one hundred and sixty-two pounds and six feet in height to continue being a defenseman and switched him to right-wing before settling on left. Over the two years, Corrigan had increased his speed, but he remained slower than many of the other forwards—just one more struggle he had to face daily. Determination had kept him a spot on his old team and won him a place on this new one. While he might not have the speed, he was a banger at assists. He wouldn't permit some bigot to destroy his dreams on the first day of practice by allowing anyone to see how they'd gotten under his skin. *Restraint.*

"That may be," Coach Massey agreed, making eye contact with Corrigan. "So, what would you suggest we do about it?"

Theriot parted his lips to respond.

"Iron crosses," the coach answered for him.

"Excellent idea. Everyone line up at the goal. Iron cross to the other end and back. Let's go."

A sea of groans spilled from the team, and DeSevren skated onto the ice from the bench.

"What's that, ladies?" Coach Massey chirped, cupping his hand to his ear and glancing at his assistant. "Did someone insist they be allowed to do ten sets followed by suicides, Paul?"

DeSevren mock-laughed. "Sure did."

"Well, if you ladies insist, I wouldn't dare stop you," Coach Massey stated, crossing his arms against his chest.

More groans rumbled from the players. Although it had been Theriot's action and ultimately his mouth that had sentenced the team to the punishment, Corrigan received the stink eye from his teammates as everyone skated to the goal.

How was this his fault? He'd been guilty of many things gone wrong today during drills. Nerves. But this? No.

DeSevren said something to Coach Massey that the rest of the team couldn't hear.

"Everyone get ready except Ellery. You're needed in the lyceum."

Why? Am I being cut? Corrigan's innards lurched.

Players cast more seething glares in his direction

as he skated past them to the chute. *Great. Now they all think I'm being absolved from punishment.* He stepped off the ice and plodded down the chute on his walk of... what? Shame? He had no idea why he'd been summoned to the lyceum, but dragging his heels—or rather skates—wouldn't amend his having to be there.

Without bothering to change, Corrigan roamed the corridor until he came to a frosted glass door with Lyceum written in scripted, etched lettering. Had this been a television game show, he may have been granted an option to choose a door or walk away with what he had. Under those circumstances, he knew what his choice would have been. Instead, he sighed and entered.

Corrigan opened the door and was taken aback for a second. *Holy mother of South Sea pearl! What an undeniable mesmerizing male specimen*—not that he should be having such thoughts. He had enough complications without adding an out-of-his-league crush to the pile. Attitudes were changing in hockey, but not that much. Corrigan had just witnessed firsthand a few hours ago how little had changed with hockey traditionalists' mindsets. Or maybe the lack of progression was due to it being the South. Or maybe both factors—traditionalists and region—were the culprits. Or maybe it was neither.

It didn't matter the reason. At the end of the day, his closet door needed to remain deadbolted. But his hike across the universe and workout in Satan's den had left him too exhausted for this type of fool-la-la today. Ninety-eight percent of his body screamed for a hot tub and liniment oil while the remainder annoyingly twitched against his jock cup at the sight of Adonis reincarnated. And here he was standing before this exquisite demigod and looking like a garbage boat—not to mention the fetid odor wafting from his pits that could stop a Roman legion dead in their tracks.

"Mr. Ellery," the handsome man seated at the long conference table greeted as he rose and extended his hand to shake. His smile appeared cordial but didn't seem to reach his eyes, and his demeanor screamed that he'd rather be someplace else—not stuck-up but distracted. Honestly, Corrigan wouldn't have been shocked to learn the man was indeed a snob. He had the bone structure for it. Everything about him looked expensive. Hell, he even smelled expensive. The man oozed vacations in the Hamptons, private jet weekend getaways, and black credit cards with offshore accounts. Even his chiseled features and creamy skin looked as if he'd descended from a line of nobility. And Corrigan probably would have found this well-put-together man intimidating had it not been for his liquid mercury eyes with a dash of melancholy watching him... waiting.

Waiting! Oh. Corrigan tuned in.

"I'm Sacha Weymouth of Ananke Legal Associates," he continued. "I represent the Croneau Foundation."

An attorney? What the hell had he done that required an attorney? Was being late that serious? Or maybe it had been his traipsing across the lawn. Or, heaven forbid, his shortcut through the stadium.

He swallowed hard as he forced his feet to move toward the man at the table. Corrigan nodded as if the company name meant something to him. It didn't, but he'd go along with whatever was happening here. He shook Sacha's hand.

"This shouldn't take long. Have a seat." Sacha motioned to the chair across from him.

Corrigan did as requested and waited while Sacha sat and shuffled papers.

"I'm pleased to inform you that you've been awarded a Croneau Foundation scholarship."

"Scholarship?" News to him, but again... gift horse.

"Yes. Since the NCAA limits the number of university athletic scholarships that can be awarded, ULSA stretches those funds by awarding mostly partial scholarships. Each year, the Croneau Foundation offers up to four gap scholarships to athletes whose athletic scholarships do not cover the full cost of attendance. This will cover the cost of textbooks and necessary class materials such as computer software, lab equipment, art supplies, and so on. Priority always goes to students on the hockey team for the obvious reason. Your coach reached out to us and explained your financial situation."

Corrigan's expression flickered between surprise, enthusiasm, and frustration. While he could use the money since he barely had enough to scrape by for the semester, it didn't thrill him to learn that others were discussing his *situation.* He wasn't destitute—at least, not yet—and he wasn't too proud to find a part-time job. Plenty of students worked. He'd never accepted charity and wouldn't begin now. He'd rather wallow in hot coals in too-tight underwear or have his toenails peeled off with a dirty paring knife first.

Except scholarships weren't exactly charity. He

would at least listen to what this dazzling human with the sexy voice and Cajun accent had to say.

"We just need to finalize everything."

Sacha's smile broadened, and Corrigan could have sworn all the oxygen dissipated from the room. The way his chest constricted, he'd gamble that better breathing conditions could be found in a diamond mine. And the way Sacha's eyes sparkled in the overhead lighting caused Corrigan's libido to run amuck. Was he an asshole for ogling and objectifying this man? Probably. But the eyes liked what the eyes liked. However, Corrigan preferred to call it appreciation.

Sacha's lips moved and then stopped.

Oh. I'm supposed to answer.

Collecting his brain cells from wherever they'd fled, Corrigan tuned back in to the present. "Sorry," he replied, flushing a splotchy red. "I'm still wrapping my head around winning a scholarship. Could you repeat the last part?"

"I asked what your major is."

Corrigan's dark brows pinched. "I'm listed as general studies."

Sighing, Sacha placed his fountain pen on the table and interlocked his fingers. "General studies?"

"My advisor suggested it because I wasn't sure."

"Honestly, these advisors need to step up their game." He smiled... kind of. "This scholarship has conditions, one of which is the recipient must have a declared major. While general studies is technically a major, it's, shall we say, wanting of distinction. Is there anything you're leaning toward?"

"I'm interested in linguistics, but I don't want to teach or be an editor, so it seems pointless."

"Is there anything else?"

Corrigan shrugged. "Architecture, but I suck at math and can't draw worth shit." His cheeks flooded with color. "Sorry. I didn't mean to cuss."

"You're perfectly fine. I can't draw worth shit either." Sacha winked.

Corrigan nearly wet himself and emitted some gasping-gurgling sound. "Egads."

Calm it down, Ellery. Be cool.

Sacha's brows arched. "You okay?"

"Yeah. My advisor said lots of players get degrees in general studies."

"Only the players who don't give serious concern to preparing a contingency plan if they don't make pro. General studies is good shoptalk for the university because, face it, you're here to play hockey. That's money in their pocket for the next four years, but not if players are flunking out. Their investment in players is a free education in exchange for their athletic ability. No pass, no play. Then they'd go in the red. It's Accounting 101. General studies typically has easy classes, minimal effort to pass, and tenured professors counting down to retirement who don't give a rip one way or the other. And it's easier dealing with those professors than ones who insist all students do the work. Fifteen years ago, the university didn't even have general studies as a major. Then the university saw the benefits, and here we are."

"So you're saying it's a trash degree."

"Not at all." Sacha shook his head. "It has merits in a whitewashed type of way. It's more tedious obtaining a job with a degree that falls into the vague and elusive abyss of 'jack of all trades and master of none.' That's not especially valuable when you need a plumber or physician—someone who knows the ins and outs of a specific trade. You don't want just anyone fumbling around with your pipes. You want someone who knows what he's doing."

You can fool around with my pipes anytime. Dammit. Uh-uh. Not going there. Concentrate! "What's wrong with being well-rounded?"

"Nothing for ordinary people who won't have assumptions made about being promoted solely for the benefit of the university." He picked up the pen and tapped it against the table. "Besides, that's why tutors exist. All athletes are required to have a study hour. The team regularly provides tutors, but if that's not enough, the scholarship covers private tutoring."

"Really?"

Sacha nodded. "Moreover, all the clichés are true. You won't know what you can and can't do unless you try. Nothing worth having comes easy. Not trying is guaranteed failure. You can do anything you put your mind to. Shall I keep going?"

"No, I get it."

"I'm going to list architecture as your major on this form, but you'll have to get that switched at the registrar's office. And I'll also need a copy of your class schedule." He slid a form toward Corrigan and pointed at a blank line. "Sign here."

Corrigan quickly scanned the document and then signed.

"These," Sacha stated, removing another form from the folder, "are the conditions of the scholarship. They are nonnegotiable. You must maintain a minimum 3.2 GPA, have regular attendance in class, not have disciplinary actions taken against you by the university, maintain a position on an athletic team, and attend at least three Croneau Foundation-sponsored events during the academic year."

Corrigan watched Sacha's rosy lips move but didn't hear anything after 3.2 GPA. The number ricocheted in his brain. *Damn!* He'd be lucky to get a 2.0 considering.

"This is especially important."

Important. Right. Corrigan refocused.

"Keep your receipts. Anytime you use scholarship funds, the purchase will need to be verified as a legitimate expense."

"So no drugs or hookers."

Corrigan didn't expect the laugh that tumbled from the lawyer. Instead of being silky smooth, it was deep and rough.

"Exactly." Sacha leaned back in his chair. "If you need something and think it's not covered, call or make a pass by the law center on campus. Someone there can answer any questions you may have."

"Make a pass?"

"Sorry. I forgot you're not from around here. It means to come by." He waited until Corrigan signed the document before continuing. "And there's one more thing."

Sacha rolled his succulent lips as he thumbed through more papers, and the tiny hairs on Corrigan's neck sprang up while his satiric meter rose another degree.

"The Croneau Foundation is a multifaceted organization that's highly visible and prominent in the community, and scholarship recipients should be a reflection of that."

Uh-oh. What shoe is about to drop now?

"And what better way to do that than by being a member of a Panhellenic fraternal group?" Sacha continued.

Fraternity? Every *National Lampoon's Animal House*, *Revenge of the Nerds*, *Alpha House*, and *National Lampoon's Van Wilder* stereotypic frat guy cliché instantaneously popped into Corrigan's mind. What the hell would he look like running around draped in a sheet with a bunch of weeds stuck in his raven hair? Wasn't the world over the whole macho guzzle from a keg and puke and whack on the ass with a wooden paddle scene?

"Rush? I have to pledge?" *Say it isn't so.* Corrigan's jaw dropped. That was so not what he expected to hear.

"I believe it's called intake now."

"Aren't fraternities expensive?"

"The foundation covers the monthly dues."

Sure, Corrigan needed the scholarship, but

joining a fraternity? He needed that as much as he did a brain bleed. No way. The idea reeked of body funk and bad decisions. This gift horse was rapidly transforming into a donkey.

"I don't think I'm the fraternity type."

"And what type is that?" Sacha asked with an edge.

Arrogant. Shallow. Materialistic. Rich. Non-inclusive. "I don't know," Corrigan answered, shaking his head and not wanting to admit his true thoughts.

"You shouldn't stereotype. There are nineteen chapters on campus. I'm positive you'll connect with some house."

"Really?" Some people required being connected to a ventilator, but Corrigan didn't fancy that idea either.

Sacha shifted in his chair and nodded as if he understood. Something in the gleam in his eyes changed as if viewing Corrigan for the first time. For a moment, Corrigan thought he detected a flicker of non-lawyerly interest but questioned if his imagination had galloped deep into the land of lunacy.

"I could write you a recommendation to my fraternity if you like."

"And say what? You don't know me."

"I know you're here. That's something."

"I'm sure none of them would be interested in me. Isn't there something else I could join? An intramural club maybe?" *Something less segregated?*

"It's nonnegotiable, Mr. Ellery." Sacha studied him for a moment before continuing. "Certain stipulations have been added to ensure that the NCAA doesn't consider the foundation scholarships to be duplicitous bribes from boosters. In short, it allows the university to have credible deniability of wrongdoing by allowing the university to argue that these are Panhellenic stipends and sponsorships should anything be questioned. It's a safeguard for the university and the recipients."

Corrigan dropped his gaze to the floor.

"What is it?" Sacha inquired.

Corrigan shrugged. "This isn't exactly how I imagined things would be."

Sacha nodded slightly. "It never is."

After a longer pause than necessary, Corrigan exhaled. "So, that's it?"

"Yes." Reaching inside his suitcoat pocket, Sacha retrieved a glossy metal case, opened it, and removed a foil business card. "Here's my card. You can call or text me anytime." He stood and extended his hand.

Corrigan stood as well, took the business card, and reluctantly accepted the handshake—not because he felt any animosity or slight toward Sacha but, rather, he was strangely disappointed that their time had come to an end.

4

SACHA

"I don't get it," Xyla griped, spooning Hollandaise sauce on her roasted asparagus. "How can you be indifferent regarding if your client is innocent or not?"

"Because it's irrelevant. Innocence and guilt are a sliding scale," Sacha responded.

"Right and wrong are absolute."

"Oh, really? Miss me with that." Sacha darted a raised eyebrow at his *date* and wondered how this conversation had arrived at where it was. He certainly hadn't brought up his job or anything close to it. The last thing he wanted to engage in was a tête-à-tête defending his profession after his fall from grace without a prospect of redemption in sight. A unanimous executive order from the firm partners had already handed off the appeal of his last case to one of his colleagues, and he'd been designated to the academia hell of preparing course syllabi for the fall semester and acting as a carrier pigeon.

The only half-decent part of his day had been meeting with Corrigan Ellery. Sacha had gone to the PAC with the expectation to get the necessary paperwork signed and nothing more, but, instead, he'd seen something in Corrigan's eyes—something that had made him pause. Most of Sacha's clients strolled arrogantly into a room, even when they were steeped chin-deep in up-the-creek situations. When he was in college, jocks had been some of the most egotistical people he'd had the misfortune of encountering. But something about Corrigan seemed different. His intense, dark eyes seemed weighted and lost—sentiments not unfamiliar to Sacha. On the other hand, what did he know? It wasn't like they'd deep-dived into a riveting, life-altering conversation. Yet Sacha had found his mind drifting back to the hockey player throughout the day and growing curious when he shouldn't have been.

"Yes," Xyla continued, her lips turning downward. "Anyone who says otherwise has questionable morals."

"Anyone who believes that is unlucky in thinking," Sacha refuted.

Gretchen placed a platter of yeast rolls on the table and plastered on one of her famous charming smiles she reserved for terse situations with patrons. "Fresh out the oven," she stated, the intention to change the conversation not disguised in her tone.

Sacha didn't bite at the out.

"Two people have a telephone conversation. Person A calls Person B and discloses an elaborate plan he's developed to murder Person C and dispose of the body. Person A has taken active steps to put his plan in motion, including purchasing a weapon, disguise, and chemicals to clean up. Person B is a known pathological liar who knows no one will believe him and tapes the conversation without Person A's knowledge in a state that requires two-party consent."

"Come on, Sacha," Paxton interrupted. "This is supper, not Intro to Criminal Justice."

Sacha ignored his brother. "Before executing his plan, Person A becomes aware of the recording, aborts the plan, and destroys all the materials he'd purchased.

There are no other corroborating witnesses to Person's A intention. Person A then goes to the police to press charges. So, should Person B be prosecuted for illegal wiretapping despite the recording being what prevented a murder? And because the only evidence of the crime is illegally obtained, is Person A criminally guilty of plotting to commit murder?"

Xyla's bottom lip jutted out in a pout. "That's different."

"No it's not. Either way, I would be defending a person who is guilty, technically speaking. And that's the thing about the law. It's not always about innocent or guilt. It is about justice and due process, which are not the same. Just because a person has good intention does not necessitate that it will reflect positively in their favor."

"Wine?" Gretchen asked.

Xyla scoffed. "Well, that's an irrational and ludicrous disservice to the people and a mockery of this country's principles."

Sacha raised an eyebrow. "You're calling my job cretinous and me iniquitous?"

"Aw, look at you using those dictionary words." Paxton passed a serving bowl of mushroom risotto to Sacha, practically shoving it beneath his nose.

"*Mais* talk about, she isn't," he refuted, the tension in his jaw obvious.

"So, you defend anyone, no matter how evil, as long as they can pay?" Xyla asked. "That doesn't sound scrupulous in the flimsiest sense."

"Sometimes Lucifer has to make his rounds in the underworld," Sacha replied.

"Oh, Jesus," Paxton muttered.

"No, I haven't gotten to Him yet."

"Anyone care for garlic butter?" Gretchen asked. "It's hand churned."

Sacha continued. "You're naive about how the law works. It's 'justice for *all*.'"

Xyla's eyes widened, clearly stunned.

"And speaking of justice," Gretchen interjected before anyone responded, "Justine Casey asked that we cater the Le Debut des Jeunes Femmes de la Sainte Anne."

Paxton smiled at her. "That's great, honey. It's the perfect opportunity to showcase your new menu."

Gretchen nodded. "Yes, and also for Xyla. She makes the most amazing champagne sabayon steak carpaccio with Ossetra caviar."

"It's raw," Sacha emphasized.

Gretchen's frown returned, and Paxton kicked Sacha beneath the table.

Oof!

"I mean, sounds delicious," Sacha reluctantly added. "Who doesn't love a good case of salmonella and *fwa*?"

Paxton kicked him again.

Fuck, dude! He rubbed his shin.

"He's joking," Paxton said with a nervous laugh. "His sense of humor is a little… discoloring."

Sacha brought his wineglass to his lips. "Some would call it *bruising*."

"It's fine." Xyla smiled. "Not everyone has a sophisticated palate that appreciates food delicacies."

"That's me. Rudimentary and unrefined." He swiveled swiftly in his chair, dodging a third blow from his brother. *Ha!* Only to be kicked in his other shin by his sister-in-law. *Ow! Damn!*

"Actually, Sacha is taking a sabbatical from criminal law to help us at the university," Paxton stated tersely.

"Well, that's one way to put it," Sacha muttered into his wineglass, doing little to mask his scowl. If his fate was to be damned to a classroom, at least it could have been defense, civil, or hell, even corporate. But no. He was reprimanded with contract law, the most boring of all fields of law in his opinion. It had been the only class he'd struggled in—not because he found the work difficult but because he barely managed to get through the required readings without falling asleep. If it hadn't been for Paxton's excellent note-taking and the OCD packrat's need to hang on to every scrap of paper he'd ever scribbled on, Sacha may have never completed the course.

Of course, Sacha knew Paxton lending him his notes hadn't been completely selfless and without motive. His intent had been to tempt Sacha into specializing in contract law alongside him. For Sacha, it had been the means to an end. He'd rather have his nose hairs plucked than ever read another tort. Just thinking about having to do so broke him out in pure meat sweats. Stubbing his pinky toe on a table leg held more appeal. While he couldn't comprehend his brother's fascination with the work, he could respect his passion for it. After all, Sacha felt the same when in front of a jury. Besides, there had been no ill will in Paxton having given Sacha a small nudge in a direction if his younger brother had seemed a smidgen lost in the sauce. That's what Sacha had done today with Corrigan... kind of.

Okay, so it had been more of a shove than a nudge, and Sacha didn't know for sure if Corrigan was bewildered about an appropriate career path. What he did know, from what he'd read on the application in the file, was that a major in general studies didn't appear to be in Corrigan's best interest. True, the application didn't tell the whole story —likely because it had been completed by Coach Massey—but it told enough to give Sacha some insight. A hockey college freshman at twenty who hadn't played in the juniors had to have some kind of story, right?

Plus, there were plenty of hockey schools in the Northeast. There had to be a reason Corrigan had selected one so far away. Then again, maybe not everyone appreciated being a homebody like Sacha. Some people enjoyed traveling. Sacha enjoyed traveling, just not alone, which was what occurred the majority of the time. It wasn't drawing the odd stares when eating in restaurants alone or being seated next to strangers on bus tours that created a pit of loneliness in him. It was seeing something amazing and having no one to share the moment. It was feeling profound and having no one to tell. It was waking up alone in a strange place. Even misery loved company.

He shrugged at his thoughts and cut into his salmon.

"Right?" Paxton asked, and Sacha realized the question was directed at him.

"*Fo sha*," he said, zoning back in and hoping like hell he hadn't agreed to something he'd regret. He shoveled a forkful of salmon into his mouth and chewed slowly. He rationalized he wouldn't be expected to speak with his jaws crammed full.

The conversation continued around him, and he attempted to focus. Honestly, he tried. Something about a science fiction movie premiere. Something else about getting stains out of tablecloths. And maybe something about mattresses. Or perhaps they had said waitresses. Or maybe it was paintbrushes. Hell, he didn't know.

He glanced at Gretchen, who still brandished an uneasy expression. Thus he didn't need to look at Paxton to know his brother was harboring a deep frown. If there was one thing Sacha knew for certain, it was when Gretchen wasn't happy, neither was Paxton, and someone would be made miserable for it. He'd prefer not to be that someone.

Plastering on his best smile, Sacha turned his attention to Xyla.

"I like scallops seared in black truffles," he blurted. It was random, out of place, and off-topic at this point, and Sacha had no idea where he was going with it. But fuck, what did it matter if it got him off thin ice with Paxton and Gretchen?

And speaking of ice, maybe he should take in a hockey game or two at the university since he'd be spending his days on campus.

He enjoyed hockey. Watching skilled athletes synthesizing catlike agility and grueling speed while maneuvering on razor-sharp blades of steel *and* remaining upright on a rectangular hunk of ice despite being intermittently bludgeoned by human cannonballs at speeds upward of thirty miles per hour warmed Sacha's blood. He considered it a brutal ballet with chest protectors and shin guards instead of tutus. In court, he played a mental hockey of chasing justice through precedents and summations rather than a puck.

It had been a while since he'd attended a live game. Well, in all truthfulness, he'd technically never seen a game in person when he thought about it. The first time he'd *attended*, Kian had been so disgustingly intoxicated that he'd puked in the parking lot, and they'd never made it inside. The second time he'd purchased tickets, his date wasn't into the whole sports scene. She'd complained so much that they'd left the arena before the National Anthem. The third and final time he'd planned on going to a game, Gretchen had gone into labor, and he'd rushed to the hospital for the birth of his first niece to ensure he'd be her favorite uncle—at least in his head that was how he saw it.

Why he'd never gotten back around to attending a game, he wasn't sure. It certainly wasn't because he couldn't get tickets. He had an excellent connection to see any Civets game, and Paxton went all the time. He supposed it was one of those things that had slipped through his social life cracks.

Yes, he definitely should catch a hockey game now that he had more free time. And it had absolutely nothing to do with a Croneau Foundation scholarship recipient who had pecked at his curiosity. Well, almost nothing. In any case, that was how Sacha was going to convince himself.

Faking paying attention, he smiled at his dinner companions discussing ganache fillings—or something of the sort—while counting the minutes until the meal ended.

Why couldn't he have an uncomplicated supper like the rest of the world?

5

CORRIGAN

ASSIGNED SEATS? THEY WERE GROWN-ASS MEN. WHO thought assigned seats were a good idea?

The dining hall was packed, and most of the diners were already seated, not because Corrigan was late but rather because he'd gotten in the wrong serving line. When the coach had finally dismissed them from afternoon practice for dinner and Corrigan had seen the multiple serving lines, he thought it was a "pick a line, any line" situation and randomly chose one. Lunch had been brown bag at the PAC, so it never dawned on him that the team's nutritionist had placed him on dietary restrictions. But when he made it to the serving bar and was asked his name, he was promptly, and unceremoniously, rerouted to the end of another line. Apparently, he was deficient in vitamin D and calcium, and the coach wanted him to bulk up. While he was too light for defense, he wasn't heavy enough for offense. Again, fuck his life. So, to the special diet line he went, where his tray was prepared for him like an infant. And now he couldn't even select where he wanted to sit and eat his baked, skinless chicken, cottage cheese, yogurt, and a clump of something that masqueraded as dessert. If he weren't so damned hungry, he'd throw his tray in the trash and head to bed. After the day he'd had, he'd have no problem crashing. But his rumbling stomach was screaming, "Feed me," like Seymour in *Little Shop of Horrors*. The irony that he was chin-deep in his self-created shop of horrors didn't elude him.

Corrigan inhaled and kept walking past plates heaped with hunks of fried chicken and mounds of mashed potatoes with flowing gravy. Restraint was something he possessed. He'd developed maturity well beyond his years. He'd had no choice. He wasn't some naive eighteen-year-old to be discounted. At almost twenty-one, he carried the burdens of a forty-year-old and had done so since he was twelve. But just because he'd become well versed in the art of refrainment didn't mean it was easy or he wasn't tempted. He had to dig deep.

Bright recessed LED lighting illuminated the cafeteria like a stadium. Oddly, Corrigan found the harsh glow soothing—familiar, reminiscent of the one in the Upstate Medical Arena at the Oncenter War Memorial. And what an arena that was. Often, he daydreamed of playing professionally there one day before advancing to the big time, racing up the ice alongside his idols with thousands of fans chanting his name and waving those annoying cheap pompoms the arena armed the crowd with for free. But then he reminded himself of the less than one-in-one-thousand chance of that happening to ground himself and remember how important this opportunity he had was. *Baby steps.* The odds of his dream developing into a reality improved by being on a college team, where scouts came to recruit and had connections with coaches. Therefore, his remaining on the coach's good side held the utmost importance.

He wasn't sure how the alumni situation worked, but it couldn't hurt to have current players on professional rosters pulling to have players from their alma mater succeed them. Plus, when he was informed that he'd been awarded the Croneau Foundation scholarship, he hadn't stopped to think what it meant. Although he'd never heard of the scholarship or the foundation, he had heard of hockey great and billionaire Timothée Croneau. Corrigan wasn't 100 percent certain that Timothée was associated with the scholarship, but surely the name wasn't a coincidence, especially given that Timothée was a Louisiana native.

Two walls were painted with murals of football players and the third with basketball, soccer, volleyball, baseball, track, and hockey players. *Nice to see such an even distribution of recognition of various sports,* he thought as he navigated his way through the maze of bodies, especially since more ULSA basketball, soccer, and hockey players had made pro teams than the football players. And if Corrigan was being honest—no bias in his opinion, of course—the football team's overall stats weren't that impressive with a 662-527-93 win-loss-tie record. In the school's history, the team had only won eleven of its twenty-four bowl games and boasted one national championship. But just to piss on that golden crown, that championship had been won before penicillin was invented. In contrast, the hockey team had over nine hundred wins, forty-five playoff appearances, and six national championships despite not being established at the school for nearly two decades later. Incontestably, the hockey team had the best record, next to gymnastics, than any other school sport. That, in Corrigan's opinion, should have elevated the hockey team to more than a scrunched parchment of wall. Again, he reminded himself where he was and dismissed the thought.

Although classes wouldn't begin for another two weeks, the majority of the university's athletic teams were holding camp. With one glance around the room, Corrigan could practically predict who belonged to what sports group. On his way into the dining hall, he'd passed the soccer team having a leisurely dinner on the knoll beside the three-tiered marble fountain with a granite statue of the school mascot towering on top. The baseball team was the closest to the entrance doors, and all wore their caps backward, and the wrestlers all donned buzzed haircuts and T-shirts with the sleeves ripped off as they gathered closest to the dessert buffet. The basketball players sat at tables located on top of the split level that were elevated higher than the others in the room to accommodate their height. Damp hair and flip-flops, not to mention the scent of chlorine, made the swimmers easy to identify. However, he couldn't differentiate between the golfers and tennis players. They both modeled striped or checkered polos and matching shorts. Of course, the gods of the university, the football players, were the easiest of all to spot in their jerseys and their premier seats in the center of the cafeteria. They were also the loudest group.

Carrying his dinner tray, Corrigan weaved through the tables of the athletic dining hall. According to his lunch card, he was assigned to table thirty-two, which turned out to be beside the glassed patio and farthest away from the drink fountains and return tray windows. Blackout curtains had been lowered to block the view of the outside world. And if the day couldn't get any worse, already seated at his assigned table were Shade Franley, Reid Larousse, and king asshole himself, Ramsey Theriot among other players.

With his eyes averted, Corrigan headed for a vacant seat at the end of the long table.

"Hey, man, where are you going?" Bowen Nguyen asked, snagging the hem of Corrigan's shirt as he passed. His smile was wide, bright, and... inviting, as opposed to the others at the table, who either looked baffled or horrified but said nothing. "Grab a piece of furniture." He jerked his head toward the chair on his right.

"I don't want to interrupt."

"Nah," Nguyen continued. "We're bitching about the first day of camp."

Larousse, goalie, dragged his hand through his coiffed haircut, pushing it away from his face. "Surely Coach can't keep this up all season. My glutes feel like I've been bashing against a hedgehog."

"Dude, tell your girl to shave," Franley heckled, bringing a round of laughs. His hair looked more orange than red beneath the lights.

"Bite me," Larousse heckled back.

"What we talking about?" Billy Idol's doppelgänger, Roland Cardenas, asked, approaching the table.

"Larousse's ass," Theriot replied.

"We're not talking about my ass."

"I stand corrected. His girl's beaver."

Another round of laughs exploded from the table.

Cardenas smirked, his braces glinting between his lips. "Y'all stupid. Larousse doesn't have a girl. An inflate-a-fuck maybe."

"I can't stand any of you," Larousse replied, feigning anger and doing his best to stifle a grin.

"Have a seat before your yogurt melts," Nguyen insisted, nudging the chair beside him from beneath the table with his foot.

Corrigan looked at the dairy cup on his tray and wondered if Nguyen knew something he didn't. After all, it was regular yogurt and not frozen. Nothing should be melting.

As much as he didn't want to accept the invitation, he equally did not want to offend the one teammate who behaved affably toward him.

I can do this. With an inward sigh, he set his tray on the table and sat.

The table grew quiet with awkwardness.

Focus on eating. Corrigan poked at the dessert blob with his spoon and watched it jiggle. Against his better judgment, he sniffed it and screwed up his face. It smelled of mint and mothballs—like the sticky candy he'd find stuck to the inside bottom of his granny's purse.

"Why do you look so miserable?" Cardenas—the one person who seemed oblivious to the mood—asked, unwrapping his silverware from the napkin and breaking the silence.

Larousse grunted. "I'd be miserable, too, if I had to eat that." He motioned toward Corrigan's tray.

"I'm not," Corrigan denied.

"You know," Theriot said, twisting his fork in his half-eaten mashed potatoes, "if Ellery could keep up, your ass wouldn't be feeling like a pincushion."

"If you would skate the plays as laid out instead of doing your own thing and being all over the ice with your head up your ass, I would be in position."

Theriot shook his head and twisted his face as if he'd bitten into something rancid. "Naw, you're just slow as fuck."

Skating speed wasn't a fixed attribute and could be improved with dedication, persistence, determination, and hard work. Being an asshole wasn't as easily overhauled.

"Theriot, chill, bro. It's the first day," Nguyen interjected. "He hasn't had time to get used to us."

Unlike football where players huddled between plays to determine their next move, nearly everything about hockey was on the fly, and teammates needed to share a brainwave. The pace and intensity didn't allow time for hesitation. Corrigan shouldn't have to guess what any of his linemates were doing; he should be able to read their body language and follow. Yes, it was only the first day, and he hadn't had much time to learn the other players' instincts and defaults, but when the coach dictated the play to skate, it eliminated all guesswork. Again, simple.

And yes, he understood he would have to step up his skate game. Yet he also knew that practice was not at the high speed of an actual game to allow the team to develop new skills and play patterns and to get used to working together as a *team*. Novel concept. So no matter how anyone wanted to contort it, Theriot's problem with him had nothing to do with hockey.

"Why are you taking up for this—"

"This what?" Corrigan snapped, the anger that had never quite subsided from earlier attempting to boil to the forefront. "Say it."

Theriot snarled, his eyes never leaving Corrigan. He clipped his sentence and stood, taking his tray. "Fucking quotas," he grumbled, heading for the exit.

Chairs scraped across the floor as most of the others at the table team followed the captain.

Cardenas glanced over his shoulder at his departing teammates and cut into his meatloaf. "Don't worry about Theriot," he reassured. "He can be a bit of a dick sometimes. He doesn't mean anything by it."

Corrigan's scowl deepened. People like Theriot he could appreciate on a certain level. At least it was upfront and allowed Corrigan to know what he was dealing with. However, people like Cardenas perpetuated the behavior by minimizing or not acknowledging it for what it was. Of course Theriot had meant something by it. The message had been loud and clear and had been cosigned by the majority of the team.

Quota. That stung, because as much as he didn't want to admit it, Corrigan had to suck down the possibility that it may have been partially true. The team had six players graduate in the spring, two to transfer, one recovering from elbow surgery, two out indefinitely on academic probation, and one to enter the draft. ULSA was certifiably in a rebuilding situation and had lots of room on the roster to fill. Corrigan had convinced himself that Coach Massey had recruited him because he was a top-notch player. But suppose he'd just needed warm bodies, and Corrigan was filling a slot until someone better came along?

And that was the kind of thought that, when it crept in, would get him booted from the team—the type that people like Theriot provoked and, if allowed, would root deep in one's subconscious and spread like cancer. If anyone thought Corrigan would sit idly by to be a placeholder, the joke was on them. He intended to be a starter despite that being a longshot for a freshman. That meant doing whatever it took, beginning with….

A final sigh escaped his lips before he scooped his spoon into the pile of cottage cheese. If that was what the coach wanted, then he'd hold his breath and swallow.

"So, you got a girl?" Nguyen asked, his smile still wide.

Momentarily, Corrigan's chest constricted with panic as his pulse thumped in his ears. Thankful to have his mouth full, he shook his head. There was no chance in hell he'd be able to swallow.

"Well, don't worry. There are plenty of honeys here."

Nope, nope, and nope. The school had zero tolerance for discrimination by students, professors, or other university staff. Yeah, well, Corrigan had seen how well that policy was taken seriously and enforced. While Nguyen appeared cool with the race thing, bringing in sexuality was entirely next level. Race was apparent. Anyone looking at Corrigan immediately recognized him to be African American. He had to do nothing and say nothing. One couldn't look at a person and know that person's sexuality. They may guess or speculate, but there was no way to know for certain unless the person confessed. A built-in gaydar was a myth, especially considering sexuality was on a spectrum and not black-and-white.

Corrigan was comfortable being a gay man, in

general, but not in the world of hockey. Not on this team. Not with these teammates who would likely become all types of weird about showering and undressing in the same room as him, fearing he'd check them out or, heaven forbid, hit on them. Hockey players were notorious for regarding themselves as an irresistible gift of manna from the heavens. Even if they weren't homophobic, their ego wouldn't allow them to dream it to be conceivably plausible that a gay man wouldn't be interested. Because, of course, gay men from the beginning of creation were desperate for dick and survived solely to flip straight guys—not.

Besides, there was no rule demanding he tell anyone. Hockey would one day, hopefully, be his profession. And everyone knew it was a good business practice to have definite boundaries between one's personal and professional life. He was simply protecting his future professional portfolio—or at least that was what he was convincing himself today. When he was younger, coming to terms with his feelings, he'd wished he was straight because he knew it would have made his life easier. He didn't intend to hide it, but he didn't intend to discuss it either. Instead, he chewed his *scrumptious* cottage cud... uh, cheese... slowly.

Additionally, there was something about "coming out" that Corrigan found repulsive and resentful. Quote-unquote straight people didn't find themselves in positions of having to announce to the world their "straightness." Their sexuality was assumed and accepted. But why should anything be *assumed*, and why wasn't all accepted? Why were only members of the LGBTQIA+ community required to rent a billboard to proclaim a part of their lives which should be private? Why must he explain or defend who he was? Corrigan felt like a Billie Holiday song: "Ain't Nobody's Business If I Do." That being said, he knew there were members of the gay community who felt everyone needed to be out regardless of whether the individual wanted to be or not, and they made it a mission to out others on the regular. A person needed to live their truth, they argued. But the truth was the world was an ugly place with an even uglier past. There were consequences, and not everything was fair.

"Mm." Larousse nodded. "Just be sure to wrap it up. Double wrap if you must. Most chase after the pigskins or the screech courts, but there's a fair share of puck bunnies scheming how to latch on and deplete your paycheck once you go pro. They're pretty sly too."

"I'm here to play and not looking to hook up or anything."

Larousse crooked his brow but didn't look up from his meal. "You training to be a priest or something? Four years is a long time to go without nooky."

"Nooky?" Stirring his tea, Nguyen grinned. "What, are you ten and never built your vocabulary? And not everyone's a manwhore like you. Besides, he didn't mean four years of being sexually comatose."

But that was exactly what Corrigan meant when it came to women.

"Only that it isn't a top priority at the moment." Nguyen gave Corrigan a reassuring nod as if to say, *I got your back.*

Cardenas twisted his face in mock scorn. "I'm disappointed in you. Slut-shaming is so 1980."

"Yes, and you know because you were born decades later. Okay." Nguyen turned back to Corrigan. "Don't worry. If you find a honey who seems sketch and none of the guys on the team already knows, Gils, the athlete trainer, keeps a list—Ditch-A-Bitch—in his office. These are babes known to have made the rounds and who attempted to pull fast ones, regardless of sport. But be careful when asking him. He snitches regularly to Coach, and

Coach thinks girlfriends are a distraction and bumping uglies on game weeks drains your energy."

"Truth. He's a stickler on curfew," Larousse added. "On away games, he posts hall monitors by the elevator to ensure no one is entering or leaving rooms."

"Don't worry about that either. You'll find there are a few ways around it."

As Nguyen continued relaying information on the dating scene, Corrigan began regretting that he hadn't gone along with the idea of him having a girl back home and being a faithful boyfriend, as it was obvious he was expected to get laid regularly—not that he would have any issues with a roll in the hay. Hell, he could use one currently to burn off some steam and relax. On the other hand, he was bored of meaningless hookups—not that he was looking to settle down.

The matter was as complicated as a fucking SAT problem. Hookups were fine. They served a purpose. They allowed him to get his jollies and move on. However, they denied him the ability to be his full self and have a support system that he wouldn't have with others. They weren't interested in having profound conversations.

But having a steady meant outing himself, something he had already determined he wasn't ready to do. In the past, he'd lost friends. In fact, he'd lost his best friend of eleven years because of it. He'd had camp coaches who'd merely suspected he wasn't straight to bench him or send him home early. Although he had an awesome family, he couldn't saddle them with any of his shit when there were flare-ups.

Now, far from New York, where no one knew him, he had a fresh start. Yes, he felt it was yet another copout, but when compared to the alternatives, it was the lesser of the evils.

Looking at his two teammates, his spirit sagged. While Larousse was a coin toss for friendship, Nguyen had seemed like a guy he could gel with and be himself around. However, after this conversation, his confidence in that had faded. His mood dipped even more when he realized just how much he wanted a friend.

Corrigan nodded again at whatever Nguyen had said and kept eating to speak as little as possible. Saying nothing wasn't a lie—not exactly the truth, but also not an overt falsehood. After all, it wasn't his fault if people made erroneous assumptions.

6

SACHA

WHAT A DISASTER. SACHA SWIRLED HIS DRINK IN HIS glass as he sank farther into the cushy Chesterfield chair. Thank God supper had concluded and he'd been able to escape to Paxton's mancave for refuge.

"That went well," Paxton stated with a broad grin.

Where? Sacha's scowl deepened. "On what planet?"

Paxton stared at him wide-eyed, his grin instantly transformed into a taut line. "You don't think so? She was totally into you, even with your grumpy, constitutional framer impersonation."

Sacha groaned. Many women were into him... for his bank account and social status. By all means, he was a "good catch," as some would put it, blessed with a pleasant appearance and an above-average

IQ. And for those reasons, many women tended to overlook his crappy attitude in lieu of a country club membership. Yes, he was well aware his disposition wasn't always skyrocketing sunshine rays out his anus, but he also didn't always recognize when he'd fallen into that vault of foulness. That was why he needed people like his brother to shake him back to reality from time to time.

"Fine." Paxton threw his hands in the air. "What's wrong with this one?"

"Nothing."

"Then what's the problem?"

"That *is* the problem. Nothing's wrong with her, but nothing's right about her either."

"I'm not understanding."

"Do you think she's the type of woman Mother and Father would approve of me bringing home?"

Paxton's face grew red. "Don't you dare tell me you're judging because she's not some socialite."

Sacha stiffened, knowing he needed to stifle his brother's defensiveness before the conversation went south and turned into a brawl.

"You know I'm not like that. What I mean is I should be with someone who at minimum checks one box."

"Huh?"

"You know how Grandmother Esmée said after Grandfather Percival died that she stopped looking for a man who would check off all the qualities she wanted in a husband and settled for one who could meet at least one of the criteria so she would, at minimum, have a companion acceptable to others."

"Whoa!" Paxton held up his hand. "First, Grandmother Esmée swallows her tobacco. Those brain cells aren't firing like they used to. Second, why would you consider that?"

"I know it's foreign to you because you've found your soul mate. But if I'm not going to have that kind of thing, then I should choose someone everyone else finds acceptable, right?"

"You're making me think you don't have all the french fries in your kid's meal. That's the dumbest shit I've ever heard you utter, and you've said some pretty stupid shit over the years."

"Is it?"

"Listen, when Grandmother Esmée lost Grandfather Percival, she wasn't ever interested in finding another great love. He was her everything, and her heart never healed. I think she thought remarrying would seem like she was trying to replace him, and that's why she settled for something less. But that's not you. You haven't had that grand love yet, and it's wrong for you to give up. And if you're trying to find a woman only to appease Mother and Father, you're going to make yourself miserable. Trust me. I went down that path, and it's like crawling on shards of glass. Besides, in the end, they came around to accept Gretchen."

Yeah, because her brother is— Let it go. He took a swig of his whiskey and sighed. "Yeah."

"Perhaps you should focus on what you want in a relationship." Paxton plopped into the chair across from Sacha. "So, what is it that you want?"

"I don't know. Someone who makes me feel less dead."

"You feel dead?"

"Yeah, unless I'm in a courtroom, which I'm not anymore. There I have a purpose and feel energetic and challenged. It's like I walk in and start connecting with people—the jury, witnesses, the judge, and even the prosecuting attorneys. They listen, and what I say matters." He shrugged. "Well, most of the time. And while no day is ever the same, there's a predictability about it." Wincing, he finished his drink. "I know it doesn't make sense."

"No, it's starting to, but…." He hesitated while contemplating. "You're saying you've never dated anyone who's mentally challenged you? C'mon.

What about that drop-dead-gorgeous neurosurgeon? What was her name?" Paxton snapped his fingers. "Michelle?"

"Micaela," Sacha corrected. "She was brilliant."

"But?"

Sacha hunched his shoulders. "Something was missing."

"Like what?"

"I don't know. Something. I tried to make it work." And honestly, he had.

"Well, things seemed to have been working fine between y'all until Miami. What happened?"

"More like what *didn't* happen. She thought if I went with her to the medical convention, we could elevate the relationship to the next level. But things started falling apart the first night there. Our flight wasn't until 8:00 p.m., but a thunderstorm delayed takeoff. We sat on the tarmac for a couple hours while it passed. Then there was an issue at check-in. By the time we got to the room, I was exhausted. She wanted to fool around, but I'd already worked a full day. All I wanted was some food because they didn't serve supper on the flight, and I'd missed lunch, a hot bath, and sleep."

Paxton nodded. "Understandable."

"Not to her, it wasn't, and it got worse. Before

takeoff, we had developed a plan—I would hang out while she attended her lectures, and then we'd meet up later to do stuff. I suggested jet skiing, aquarium, botanical gardens, museums. Her only interest was sex."

"Not many men would complain about that."

"Only when it's good."

Paxton snorted. "Bruh, it's always good, even when it's bad."

"If you say so."

"I hate to ask this, but what made it... not good?"

"It just wasn't. A similar thing happened with Stacey and Brie. And Kendra. The conversation was popping, but the deed was flopping."

"Hmm." Paxton rolled his lips and remained quiet for several seconds. "Has this always been the case?"

Sacha contemplated for a moment before nodding. "Pretty much."

"So, you don't enjoy sex?"

"I do. I mean, I would," he stammered. "I want to."

"But you haven't?"

"Not with another person." As the confession left his lips, his dignity plunged into the toilet. "Frankly, there's been a few times when I couldn't... you know... finish properly. I've seen doctors, and they say there's nothing wrong with me physically, that perhaps I was overly fatigued or had consumed too many adult libations."

"Sacha…." Paxton set his glass on an end table and leaned forward. "Have you ever considered that you're not into women?"

What! Holy shit, Sacha hadn't seen that coming, and it took another moment before he was able to translate the thought into verbal speech. "What?" His voice hitched. "Of course I'm into women." Wasn't he? Sure. Stupid question.

Right?

"It's okay if you're not."

"What the absolute fuck?" Wouldn't he already know this? Wasn't he a little old to be discovering his sexuality? Wasn't there like some cutoff or expiration date or timestamp for sexual epiphanies?

His throat dried as doubt seeped in.

"I'm just asking."

Well, you don't need to. "Why would you jump to the conclusion that because I've never had a mind-blowing sexual experience"—*oh shit!*—"that I don't like women?" As he concluded the sentence, his confidence dropped even further.

"Well, clearly something's going on."

Put that way, yeah. Sacha stared over his glass with his mouth hanging open at his brother. Speechless. He placed his hand on his abdomen to soothe the trepidation clawing in his gut, threatening to bring up his honey-glazed salmon. *What's happening?* "But that? Why?"

Paxton's expression softened to one of pity.

Oh geez, not that look.

"Honestly?" Paxton asked.

Sacha nodded despite not wanting to hear the answer.

"Kian."

"Oh, because Kian is gay, I must be too?"

"Now you're overreacting." Paxton rose and went to the bar. "That's not what I said, nor what I meant." After retrieving the bottle of Little Book Chapter 5, he returned to his chair and refreshed both their drinks. "But you have to admit you were happier when you two were together."

"We weren't *together*." Sacha scoffed, his voice cracking in strange ways that it hadn't since adolescence. "He's my friend."

"You spent all your time with him."

"We hung out the way *friends* do because, you know, we're *friends*."

"Don't get defensive."

"I'm not defensive," he rebutted in a tone that

convinced no one ever. Every muscle in his body clenched.

"I never saw you more depressed than when he moved with his boyfriend to Seattle."

Sacha's bottom lip drooped in a pout. "How would you feel if your best friend moved across the country? I wouldn't imagine you'd be flipping cartwheels."

"Fair enough, but let me ask you something. You don't have to answer me, but be honest with yourself. If he had tried, would you have kissed him?"

"No." Sacha froze at his automatic response because something about it wasn't ringing one hundred with him. *Would I have?*

"You don't sound convinced." Paxton covered his brother's hand with his. "I remember one afternoon arriving home for spring break during my first year of law school. You were a senior and had friends over out by the pool. The music was blaring, and people were laughing and splashing around. But not you. You were focused on Kian and his then-boyfriend making out. Your cheeks were flushed, and you kept shifting as if you couldn't get comfortable."

"I don't remember that." *Ten Hail Marys for that whopper* as the image of the live boy-on-boy action flooded his memory. Damn if his cheeks weren't currently staining with color, causing him to want to dissolve into the floorboards.

"Then Sera Magee asked you to rub tanning lotion on her back, and you took her to your bedroom."

"To get the tan—"

"My bedroom was next to yours, remember?" Paxton interrupted. "I heard y'all. You oiled her up all right."

Ah! A reprieve. Yes, he could chalk it up to immaturity and hormones. "We were a couple of horny teenagers. Big deal. And," he drew out, "she was a girl, which doesn't support your theory."

"It does if watching Kian is what started your motor running."

As quickly as he thought he'd gained some ground, his buoyancy deflated. He swallowed past the lump in his throat. "He's my friend." *Lame rebuttal, but worth a try.*

"And if he wasn't?"

Sacha took a long sip, rubbed the throbbing center of his forehead, and sagged in the chair, afraid of the thoughts formulating. Was his brother right? His breath pulsated in his ears like thunder. Paxton's theory shouldn't be making as much sense as it did.

Oddly, the fact that he might not be sexually attracted to women wasn't what troubled him. Rather, it was his not realizing it was a possibility that shook him to his core. How could he have not known this about himself? It was like waking up and not knowing his eye color or favorite food. Sexuality was an integral part of human nature, and he just what? Got in the default line by mistake? And what was the exchange policy on this type of thing?

This wasn't how it was supposed to work. Other people didn't inform a person what that person's sexuality was. Seriously, how could Sacha not know every nook and cranny about this part of his life? After all, he was an overall observant guy, paying attention to the smallest details. It was what made him a great trial lawyer—well, until prior to the current debacle. He'd graduated in the top 1 percent of his law class. He figured out the twist ending of movies long before they occurred. He solved riddles that stumped all his friends at trivia. Yet he didn't know if he'd had a thing for guys, let alone for his quiche bestie? No, not quiche. Quiche would mean…. *Double shit!* Thoughts whirled in his mind too swiftly for him to latch on to any.

"Okay," Paxton continued, "suppose it was some other guy. How would you feel then?"

Not fair. Sacha parted his lips to speak the obvious, or rather the traditional, but then hesitated as he gave it genuine consideration. "I wouldn't be completely—" His voice shook as he fought to continue. "—opposed to it." Did he actually say that aloud? "But I'm not g-gay. I... I...."

"Don't have to figure it out right this second," Paxton soothed. "Breathe."

"But I'm not," Sacha continued. *And I doth protest too much.*

"Okay. So maybe you're not a zero on the Kinsey scale. There's nothing wrong with that. It simply gives you more options in finding your soul mate."

Great! Just what I needed to add to this flaming pile of crap day. I should have stayed at home and eaten a TV dinner.

7

CORRIGAN

CORRIGAN SKATED ONTO THE ICE WITH MINOTAUR veteran Shelby Kavanaugh and Thad Hansford, a college freshman after having aged out in juniors. Together, the three comprised the fourth offensive line. Ordinarily, this would have been a bruise to Corrigan's ego. He hadn't traveled all this way to be delegated to the fourth line. Then again, his line was far from sloppy. Kavanaugh may not have had the best form Corrigan had ever seen, but he knew how to hustle. He made plays where none were to be had. And Hansford possessed mad stickwork skills that surely were taking him places. But on the other hand, if his skills were that impressive, why hadn't the pros plucked him from the juniors? And if the coach thought Hansford was only fourth-line material with the skills he brought, what did that mean for Corrigan?

He didn't know what to make of it and shrugged off the thought as he took his position. Now wasn't the time for him to attempt to psychoanalyze his coach.

At the whistle, Theriot immediately took control of the puck and broke away across the line.

Damn, he's fast!

Corrigan chased Theriot but was checked by Sweeten, allowing Theriot to take a shot on goal before Corrigan could scramble back to his feet. Fortunately, Abe Barnes made a pad save and knocked the puck to Corrigan, who rifled past Theriot and won the race to the dot. His shot from the far circle went wide and was picked up by Hansford, who played it around the net. Corrigan took a cross-ice pass from Hansford off the left boards and snaked past Franley playing the opposing defense before lifting a shot over Larousse's left shoulder from the low slot and into the back of the net.

Yaaas!

Wham!

Ow!

For a second, Corrigan saw a flash of white light followed by darkness before focusing on fuzzy teammates. A sharp surge of what felt like a combination of scorching and constricting overtook his face.

"Jesus!" DeSevren yelled, rushing to Corrigan. "Someone fetch me a towel and some ice." He looked him over. "Are you all right?"

"Yeah," Corrigan answered as an automatic response. Although he'd heard the question, he couldn't process the meaning. His legs quivered as he skated toward the bench, and DeSevren grasped his upper arm to steady him. Corrigan's vision cleared further but was impaired by his fogged visor speckled with… blood. *What the hell?* Blood streamed from Corrigan's nose down his chin and onto his practice jersey.

"Theriot, what were you thinking?" DeSevren snapped.

"Sorry, Coach, it was an accident." Theriot's tone was 100 percent horse manure.

"Accidents like that better not happen in a game, let alone in practice against your teammate. Everyone, twenty laps, and each better be under fifteen seconds." He blew his whistle.

He hit me. The realization sank into Corrigan. Theriot had elbowed him in the face. His visor had caught the brunt of the impact but not all, not enough to prevent Theriot from bloodying Corrigan's nose.

That son of a—

Corrigan's lips pulled into a thin line, and he jerked to take off after Theriot but was held in place by DeSevren and blinded by a wadded towel pressed against his face.

"Cool your skates," Coach Massey ordered. "Theriot said it was an accident."

Uh-huh. How does one's elbow accidentally end up in another person's face beneath a protective visor?

"And you're on scholarship," Coach continued.

The latter kept Corrigan moving toward the bench. The conditions of his scholarship specified no university disciplinary actions. Fighting would most definitely fall under that category.

He clutched the towel and held it to his nose. "I got it, Coach."

Oh, and how he got it on every level. The golden boy, Theriot, was off-limits.

IF CORRIGAN HAD THOUGHT THE BEATING RAYS OF THE Louisiana summer sun on the rear of his neck were Dante's ninth circle of hell, this blustery blanket of trapped humidity beneath the stacking clouds was the tenth. He sucked in the thick air as he trudged up a hill and back to the athletic dorm from the arena since the shuttles had limited hours during the summer. He could have taken his chances and waited at the stop, but the angry clouds in the west threatened to burst at any second. Lightning skidded across the sky in the distance. His teammates had all piled into cars with no room for an additional passenger, of course. But so what? Hiking built character, right? At least today he didn't have a mound of textbooks strapped to his back. Maybe there was hope for his spine yet. Then again, what would it matter if he drowned in a flash flood and his body was washed into the Civil War trenches on either side of the road?

Okay, maybe calling the decline a trench was a bit of a stretch—or not. They were steep enough to be trenches, and several Civil War battles had been fought in the area. Plenty of statues and plaques strung across campus commemorated the events. One of the buildings—Corrigan wasn't sure which one—had been used as a war hospital for Confederate soldiers. During his campus visit, the guide had boasted about how the converted hospital had an innovative sewage system courtesy of the university engineering department. Corrigan stared at the long ditches again and frowned. Great. He'd be buried in a literal cesspool. Yet he had to admit, there was a poetic symmetry to ending a shitty day in a shithole. At least he'd have the university's chapel bells that rang in the distance to keep him company as his body lay decomposing.

A gust of warm wind, bringing with it a strong scent of wild onions, slapped against his face and tousled his hair. He squinted to shield his eyes from particles of blowing dust, because all he needed was a scratched cornea to go along with his black eye and swollen nose.

From nowhere, shimmering lights appeared far down the road and advanced. A four-door Mercedes slowed and eased to a stop on the semi-isolated *Rocky Horror Picture Show*-ish road. *Shit! The "Black people always die first in slasher films" cliché.*

This could play out several ways, with the majority of options not being favorable, especially since Corrigan hadn't taken any recent photos that wouldn't pixelate into a blurry blob when blown up for the back of a milk carton, provided that someone thought him worthy enough to be declared missing.

Wait. Are milk carton pictures still a thing since most of mainstream America seemed lactose intolerant?

Corrigan tensed as the tented passenger window —surely too dark to meet visible light transmission percentages regulations—lowered.

When Sacha leaned toward the window, Corrigan relaxed for a brief moment and then tensed again for an entirely different reason. *Fuck my life! Of course he'd roll up on a day my face imitates Kung Fu Panda.* The "killed by a madman on the side of a remote university side street" scenario he'd concocted in his mind was replaced with "kidnapped by a gorgeous demigod to be a sex slave." Actually, the second option didn't seem half bad, and Corrigan perked up marginally at the impure thought.

"Hey. Where you heading?" Sacha asked.

"To my dorm."

"Hm." He peered out his front windshield at the clouds and squeezed the steering wheel before looking back at Corrigan. "There's about to come a monsoon. You'll never make it in time. Hop in."

Corrigan shifted indecisively. Sure, his legs would thank him, and his eyes would be more than grateful to have Sacha as a view, but he despised accepting things from people. It put him in their debt and lessened who he was as a person. He was raised never to take handouts, and here, once again,

Sacha was offering him a handout. Yes, the scholarship was different but still a type of handout all the same. *He must think I'm pathetic.*

"I think I can make it."

"*Sha*, there's no way." Sacha pushed open the passenger door. "It's best to mow the lawn and cut up the snakes."

What?

Corrigan poised himself to decline again when a bolt of lightning streaked from the sky to the ground, followed by a vociferous boom. Although the lightning had been miles away, the heat had warmed his skin. In an instant, his mind was made up. Never mess with Mother Nature trumped snubbing handouts for the sake of pride. Respect.

"Thanks," he replied, stepping toward the car.

"*Pshaw.*" Sacha removed his neatly folded suit jacket from the passenger seat and tossed it over his shoulder onto the back seat without looking, then set a bottle of unopened Rhys Horseshoe Hillside pinot noir on the floorboard. "Looks like I happened along at the right time." A kind smile slid across his face.

"Yeah." As Corrigan fastened his seat belt, an awareness came over him, and his head snapped toward the radio. He couldn't suppress giggling like an adolescent.

Sacha studied him, brows furrowed, and tilted his head. "What's funny?"

"Nothing." Then he nodded toward the radio. "You're listening to 'Hotel California.'"

"The Eagles are humorous?"

Sacha listening to a band like the Eagles definitely shocked Corrigan. He'd expected him to be more of an opera or symphony music lover—smooth jazz at best—and not throwback classic rock.

"It's not that. You're on this back road... in a Mercedes...." Corrigan felt his face growing warm. "Church bells ringing...." He nodded toward his feet. "Wine."

"Ah!" Sacha grinned, accelerating. "Well, I guess you'll need to decide if you're in heaven or hell and if I'm twisted."

"This car is heaven, but this campus is definitely purgatory."

"Tough time adjusting?"

"I don't think adjusting is my problem. Some things suck no matter where you are."

Sacha nodded. "Now, that's true. Anything I can do to help?"

His offer seemed genuine, and Corrigan smiled. "Naw. I'll work it out, but thanks."

The music was interrupted by a phone ringing and the word "Incoming" appearing on the radio display. With his thumb, Sacha pressed a button on the steering wheel to accept the call. "*Quoi ça dit?*"

"Father called. He and Mother are still in Lake Charles, and the alarm is going off at the house. Security has already checked it out, and everything is fine. But someone needs to reset the alarm."

Sacha frowned. "And I suppose that *someone* is me."

"You're closer."

"You don't know that."

"*Mais*, I do. I called work, and they said you'd just left. It's on your way."

"Only if I go eighteen miles out of the way," Sacha refuted. "Do I look like the kid who ate the glue at school?"

"Come on. I'm at home with the kids. You wouldn't want me to have to drag your nieces out in this weather, would you? Say hello to your uncle, girls."

"*Salut, Nonc*," two small voices said in unison.

"*Salut, mes belles.*"

"Go wash your hands for supper," Paxton

instructed, followed by the sound of scuttling feet across a wood floor.

"Really, Pax? You're going to guilt me with your kids?"

"Is it working?"

"No."

Corrigan could tell by Sacha's expression that it totally had worked, and something inside him warmed at how quickly Sacha melted from staunch affirmation to gooey fondness.

"I'll bring you one of Gretchen's deluxe cinnamon rolls tomorrow."

Sacha licked his lips at the bribe. "With extra icing."

"Fine. You drive a hard bargain."

"Sure." Sacha disconnected and glanced at Corrigan. "I feel like a cheap pastry whore."

"Nothing about you looks cheap."

"It's the cuff links," he responded nonchalantly. "If you ever want to fool someone into thinking you have money, invest in a good pair. The eyes always find the smallest details and give them the most creditability. You can be wearing a ten-dollar suit with rummage store shoes, and people see custom cuff links and assume you're hiding your wealth. But see someone wearing a five-thousand-dollar suit and designer shoes but with dollar store cuff links, and everyone will assume that person is faking the funk."

Corrigan laughed. "Nice to know, but it isn't solely the clothes."

"Oh?" Sacha's eyebrows flew up, and he glanced from the road to Corrigan.

"It's your entire demeanor—the way you speak and move."

"Move?"

"Yes. Kinda like you're gliding, flawless."

"While I don't trip over my feet most mornings, I'm definitely not flawless, but it's entertaining that someone thinks I might be." He chuckled to himself.

"Well, you certainly don't thump around the way hockey players do."

Sacha pulled to a four-way stop and clicked his blinker. *"Humph.* You've never seen me without contacts."

"I didn't realize." There was a pause. "Are they colored?"

"What? My contacts?"

Corrigan nodded.

"No," Sacha answered.

"That's good." *Oh no, you didn't say that aloud. Goof!*

"Why is that good?" Small smile creases formed at the corners of his eyes.

"They're pretty." *Shit! Open mouth, insert foot. Save yourself.* Heat crept up Corrigan's neck. "R-Rare," he stuttered, the heat climbing into his cheeks. "They're pretty rare. Less than 3 percent of people have gray eyes."

"And you know this because...?"

"I wrote a paper about eye color for biology class last year."

"Well, heck. I thought you may be one of those people who walked around with random statistics and weird facts in their heads. I got excited for a second and was going to invite you to be my partner for the next trivia night."

Excited? Ga-geez! Pull your mind out of the gutter. "I'm not that great at trivia."

"Eh." Sacha shrugged. Fat drops of rain began pelting the windshield, and he flipped on the wipers. "You'd probably be bored with all us geriatric folks anyway."

"You're not old."

Sacha grunted. "When I was twenty, I thought thirty was ancient."

"I'll be twenty-one soon." *But for you, my throat will turn forty, open up, and say ah tonight!*

"And I'll still be thirty-two and basic AF. Do you even know what it's like to be in bed and asleep by ten? I've already found my first gray hair."

Sacha sounded so dejected that Corrigan laughed. "Gray hair makes a man look distinguished." *What the hell just fell out my mouth?* Next, he'd be declaring a daddy fetish.

Careful. This man oversees your scholarship. He blinked hard.

"Silver. Gray is trite. But silver…." Sacha wagged his finger. "Silver has charm and is on the stock exchange." He pulled the Mercedes into the parking lot of the athletic dorm and stopped at the front doors.

"Thanks for the ride." Corrigan lifted his gym bag into his lap and opened the door. "And it wouldn't matter gray or silver. You'd wear them both well."

Run.

He dashed to the building before Sacha could respond or he could swallow his entire leg.

8

SACHA

SACHA STRETCHED OUT ON THE SECTIONAL IN HIS parents' sitting room with his warmed kibbeh and toed off his shoes while he waited for the rain to slack. After passing several wrecks and hydroplaned cars off the side of the road, he'd preferred not to venture out among the *couyons* who couldn't conclude that it was wise to slow down in zero-visibility slanting rain. He especially wasn't motivated to leave when his parents' fridge and cupboards were stocked, and he was surviving off canned soup at his place until he made a grocery bill. Why adult when he could camp out here as long as his parents were away? Besides, he doubted his house had power if the storm-tracking radar was reliable. It showed his neighborhood on the grid for being in the thick of straight-line winds. Pine trees were known to snap if anyone sneezed too hard, and his gated subdivision was overrun with them—hence the name Pine Grove Estates.

Steam escaped the croquette when he cut into it with his fork, and he set it aside on a sofa table to cool. In the meantime, he scrolled through top newsfeeds on the internet before he found himself searching eye color.

If gray eyes were rare, black were rarer. He couldn't even find a percent for people with black eyes. Not brown or dark. Black. He'd inspected Corrigan's closely today, and they were indeed noir without a speck of brown. And no, he didn't mean the purple-and-black party happening on Corrigan's face... which piqued Sacha's curiosity. However, he figured inquiring would be rude, especially after Corrigan's purgatory comment. Something was definitely going on with Corrigan, but Sacha didn't know him well enough to start asking personal questions. He also didn't want to give the impression of being an ambulance chaser. Perhaps, if the ride had been longer, he would have felt more comfortable prying. Maybe their paths would randomly cross again soon. Yet he couldn't shake the feeling that his seeing Corrigan today had been purely coincidental.

He rarely drove the back road, and the only reason he'd taken that route today was to avoid driving by campus police. They had been after him to get a faculty decal for his car. But once he did that, it would mean admitting what his life had become. It meant accepting being in a classroom and not a courtroom. He couldn't. He just couldn't. Not yet anyway. So he'd taken the long way around, where he'd been certain to bump into no one. But then there was Corrigan. Who walked from there to the main campus? Had to be fate.

But okay, if it was fate, exactly what was it saying? There was a moment—a couple, actually—that Sacha thought Corrigan may have been flirting with him. However, that didn't make sense. First, no way would Corrigan be interested in anyone his age. Second, did gay hockey players exist? In theory and the rest of the world, maybe. But in Bible Belt athletics, absolutely not. Well… he'd heard parlor room rumblings about some of the players on the Saint Anne Civets, but nothing official. In fact, he was fairly certain about two, but until either made an announcement, he wouldn't assume. All that aside, third, he wasn't gay. At least, he didn't think so. Or was he? *No, not that question again.* Ever since Paxton had broached the subject, Sacha couldn't shake the idea. And the more he thought about it, the more things stacked in that direction. For example, tonight, when he'd thought Corrigan had been flirting with him, he'd enjoyed it. And he'd be lying if he denied his eyes had lingered on Corrigan's ass longer than necessary or that he'd delighted in Corrigan's fresh soap scent. Labels didn't bother him. Well, they did when he didn't know which were appropriate.

His phone rang. Glancing at the screen, he saw it was his father and elected to let the call go to voice mail. Just because he was in his father's house and eating his food didn't mean he had to take his phone calls. As an employee, he knew he should answer, but as a son, he refused. His father had grounded him, so to speak, and Sacha wasn't above behaving like a sulking child. How long he could continue avoiding phone calls was another matter. Eventually, he would need to work his way back into his father's good graces.

As the screen went dark, an epiphany struck him. He needed a second opinion. Grabbing his phone, he clicked on Kian's number in the contact list.

Kian cheerily answered on the first ring. "My dude, what's going on?"

"Have you ever thought of me as being sexually ambiguous?"

"What?" There was a loud crash as if dishes were dropped in a sink.

"You know. Have you ever thought I might not be straight?"

Kian burst into a fit of laughter. "Are you drunk?"

"I'm serious."

"Who is he?"

"Who is who?"

"The guy who has your dick all tight?"

Sacha frowned. "There's no guy." *At least not yet, anyway.*

"Don't feed me that bullshit."

"It's not—"

"Okay, then why are you asking?"

"Why are you evading?"

Kian released a long sigh. "I'm tired of this *Dragnet* conversation. Tell me what's going on."

"It's something Pax said."

"Well, it took him long enough to notice."

Sacha set erect on the couch. "What's that supposed to mean?"

"That you've always acted a bit… fluid."

"Fluid?"

"Ah, Sacha, relax. You are what you call yourself."

"I want to be who I am." The tendons in his neck constricted. Perhaps calling Kian wasn't such a good idea after all.

"Listen, I wouldn't be honest if I said I haven't ever wondered, but you never said anything, so why should I?"

"Because you're my best friend."

"Yes, and best friends don't out each other, not even to themselves." Although Sacha couldn't see him, Kian's compassionate smile could be heard in his voice. "I think you fell into a comfort zone of what was expected of you and ignored everything else."

Sacha arched his brow. "Everything else like what?"

"My gay friends would hit on you all the time, and you would flirt back subconsciously but never go all in. Flynn Pelletteri worked himself up for a month to ask you to prom, and you told him if you found a date, you'd be happy to double. You crushed him."

"That never happened. He…." Sacha abandoned his sentence as he reflected on the memory of that day with Flynn at the stables. He'd been brushing down his horse when Flynn had approached him, acting fidgety and with a flushed face. It had been brisk out, and Sacha assumed Flynn's shuffling had everything to do with the chill in the air and not…. *Oh!* He *had* asked him out, and Sacha had been too oblivious to understand. *I'm an idiot.* "I—"

"Your family laid out a road map for you, and you unquestioningly followed because you want to be a people pleaser. You may pretend not to care, but you do. The fact that you're not in a courtroom isn't what's really eating you. It's wanting to get back in there for a do-over to win back your father's graces. And you've tried to love people who others said you should love instead of trusting your instincts. So, I'll ask again. Who is he?"

Ugh! Even thousands of miles away, Kian could call him out.

"This is going to sound weird, but there's this guy… a client, kinda." *Enter ethical complications.* "I was supposed to get him to sign some papers, but something about him…. He's not what I expected."

"What did you expect?"

"Some typical know-it-all muscle brain who thinks he's the center of the universe. I mean, he may be. We haven't interacted much. But from what I've seen thus far, he seems to be a decent person."

"And someone you wouldn't mind getting to know better?"

Sacha nodded as if Kian could see. "Something like that." The saying that birds of a feather flock together came to Sacha's mind. Corrigan seemed just as lost as he was. Sacha couldn't put his finger on it, but there was something—an *umph*—about Corrigan that he connected with. When he looked into Corrigan's eyes, a tenderness stirred on his insides. It didn't make sense.

"Then take your shot."

Leave it to Kian to make such an elementary proclamation.

"It's not that simple."

"It is if you want it to be."

Sacha rolled in his lips. Was that what he wanted?

"Thing is, I don't know if he would appreciate me doing so. He's a hockey player."

"And?"

"It's not something hockey players do."

"What medieval, intergalactic, heteronormative gender roles fantasy world do you live in?"

"I know how that sounds, but it doesn't make it any less true. Remember how it was for you on the lacrosse team?"

"What I remember is having people like you who

always had my back no matter what. I remember you standing up to bullies twice your size to defend your gay friend and being the champion of those who needed it."

"Funny, I remember getting my ass kicked."

"And that never stopped you. You've never been afraid to get in there and scrap. Plus, I recall you winning your fair share of fights. You have an uncanny, innate gravitation to those who need defending whether you know it or not. Whether *they* know it or not. It's why you're so good at your job."

"Obviously not good enough."

"When are you going to stop beating yourself up about something that's not your fault? You can offer advice. You can't force people to take it."

Sacha sliced into his kibbeh again. Less steam escaped. "I guess."

"There's no guessing about it. It's fact." Kian sighed. "Listen, stop trying to be perfect."

Sacha opened his mouth to argue, but Kian cut him off.

"You go out of the way to please everyone except yourself and have suppressed parts of yourself because they don't fit a mold."

"Did you get a new job channeling Sigmund Freud?"

"Well, speaking of jobs, I hate to cut this short, but I need to bounce. The station has me covering this state welfare audit that claims $94 million have been misappropriated. Seems it's linked to an investment firm in Nevada. The governor is holding a press conference. Call you later?"

"Sure thing."

Setting the phone down and twirling his fork in his food, Sacha thought over the conversation. He wasn't sure if he had gained clarity or muddied the waters more. However, one thing had been made clear: evidently, he'd been emitting some kind of vibes for years that wasn't hitting on the straight bar. He pondered if he would have gone out with Flynn if he had realized Flynn's invitation. He liked to think he would have. But if Kian was correct in his assessment, Sacha probably would have been too concerned with his parents' opinion to have accepted. And if the latter was the case, it made him chickenshit. Only, Weymouths weren't chickenshit. They led charges and carved new paths.

Maybe I'm adopted. Ugh!

He popped a forkful of kibbeh in his mouth and leaned back against the sectional.

A social media notification appeared on his phone, and he swiped to open it. It was an advertisement for a psychic reading. Considering, he arched a brow and slowed chewing. There wasn't a limit to the number of opinions one could get, now was there?

He scrolled to the bottom of the advertisement.

Then again, $1.99 a minute sounded exactly like his limit.

9

CORRIGAN

A SECRETARY LED CORRIGAN DOWN A LONG HALL adorned with oil portraits and into a room painted a soft yellow ochre trimmed in a rich gingerbread before closing the door behind him. He glanced at the nameplate on the door—Maxwell Weymouth— as it clicked shut. Stepping forward, he took in his surroundings. As expected, it was posh with a winter white velvet-tufted sofa and two ivory fauteuil chairs to the left. A mixture of sandalwood and black coffee fragranced the air, and Corrigan almost forgot where he was or why he'd come. But the shuffling to his right dragged him back from the land of awe.

Catty-cornered across the room, a large mahogany desk occupied the space. Behind it, Sacha rose in all his handsome glory, and a chill of excitement skidded across Corrigan's skin. He hadn't expected to see him based on the name on the door.

"Corrigan." Sacha extended his hand as he stepped around the desk, his crisp pale blue shirt with white collar and cuffs fitting his torso like a second skin. His tie was silvery white with tiny blue and gold polka dots and styled with an Eldredge knot. He completed the look with navy suit pants with a sharp crease.

Always so neat and tidy.

Immediately as Corrigan's palm slid against Sacha's, a familiar jolt of electricity sparked in him. It was becoming ridiculous how easily this man punched all his stimulation buttons in the right way.

Gesturing to the sitting area, Sacha asked, "What can I do you for?"

Corrigan strode across the room and lowered himself into one of the chairs. Unzipping his backpack, he retrieved a pink sheet of paper. "My schedule, Mr. Weymouth."

"No, no." Sacha shook his head as he sat in the chair beside Corrigan. "There are far too many of those around here. I'm Sacha." As he extended his hand to accept the paper, his fingers skimmed across Corrigan's, and Corrigan sucked in his breath.

Sacha's gaze flew up from the paper, and the two locked in a stare.

Sounds from a grandfather clock tucked in a corner filled the room as the background noise to their inhaling and exhaling. How were they that close—mere inches apart? Corrigan had an urge to reach out and trace Sacha's strong jawline to his glistening lips. *Whoa! Simmer down.* Instead, when Sacha's gaze turned inquisitive, Corrigan straightened, stiffened, and inched back. *Space.* Yes, that was what he needed. However, he could will his body back no farther than he'd moved, and the two remained close. So, if he wouldn't—*couldn't*—move, he needed to speak.

"I discussed changing my major to architecture with my advisor," Corrigan said, his voice shaky. "She advised against it."

"Well, of course she did."

"It's a five-year program."

"And you plan on being pro by then," Sacha said with a pert smile.

"Hopefully. You say it as if it's a bad thing."

Sacha shifted in his chair. "Not if that's what you want, but I don't see where one thing has to do with the other."

Cocking his head, Corrigan asked, "You don't?"

"Sure, it may be tough, but plenty of people work full-time and attend college. You may have to take summer courses each year or night classes. And there's always online or remote classes."

"But on whose dime? If I don't make pro, I can't afford—"

"If you commit to the major, you can apply for an extension. We can set up an appointment, and I'll help you complete the paperwork. All you'll need is your curriculum check sheet that proves the program is designed by the university to be five years. Or another other-case scenario is if your coach decides you require more growth and development and thereby redshirts you—in which case you'd obviously remain on the team for an additional year of eligibility—that would meet the criteria for an extension as well."

Redshirted? Corrigan went pale. He'd never considered being benched his first year as an option, but it could happen.

"Are you okay?" Sacha placed his smooth hand on Corrigan's calloused one, which should have been innocent enough but wasn't.

Corrigan's stare flew to their hands and stuck while a swarm of butterflies fluttered in his stomach. *Calm yourself. Play it off. He means nothing by it. He's talking business. You can't afford to blow this opportunity, and he doesn't want you hitting on him.*

However, his self-talk went ignored by his entire limbic system, and yearning gushed through his veins like viscous lava scorching a path. He parted his lips to respond, pressed them together, and then tried again cagily.

"I'm… I'm fine." He wasn't, but for the sake of his college career, he needed to be.

Sacha

WHAT WAS WITH HIM? SERIOUSLY, WHAT WAS HIS freaking problem? He had never been touchy-feely, especially not in a professional situation. A firm handshake sufficed in most situations, and occasionally, a reassuring, quick pat on the shoulder was appropriate. But a handhold or whatever he was doing? Nothing about this was appropriate. Yet something about Corrigan compelled Sacha to make physical contact. And the most puzzling thing about his action was he wasn't making an effort to withdraw—at least, not until his stomach unceremoniously rumbled through every section of his intestinal tract. *Sexy... not.*

Hold on. Since when had he become concerned about appearing sexy? Probably about the same time a scholarship extension required a meeting and paperwork. He could download the curriculum check sheet from the university website, and technically, the paperwork required checking a box on the current application. Admittedly, he could complete all that was needed in a few minutes as they currently spoke. However, there was only one reason Sacha would have fabricated a need for another meeting. He wanted an excuse to see Corrigan again. Why? He didn't know other than he was intrigued. While their conversations hadn't been intense, they had been more kindred than any other he'd had with people not related to him. It didn't make sense. Then again, multiverse time travel didn't resonate with him, either, yet millions of people hopped on that futurology train with full understanding.

Snap out of it. He's too young. Young but legal. He's a client. But not really. Technically, it's the Croneau Foundation that Father represents. I wouldn't be brought to the ethics council, although Father might skewer me up over a spit with a Granny Smith shoved in my mouth. But hasn't he already done that? He'd do it again. Get out of your head.

The door burst open. "Sacha, I need—" Paxton halted at the doorway with a stack of thick books pressed against his chest, and the words died on his lips. His eyes zoomed in on Sacha's and Corrigan's hands clasped on the table and then darted between the two men, his brows pulling together before arching.

Oh no. Sacha recognized that look. The recovery was quick, but not before Sacha noticed.

"I thought you were alone."

And he recognized that tone—not judging but judging. If his older brother thought for a second that Sacha would be acknowledging the elephant that had just stampeded into the room, he'd be thoroughly disappointed. *Not a chance. Divert.*

Sacha leaned back in his chair, breaking hand contact with Corrigan. He nodded toward the books, his lips tugging downward at the corners. "That better not be what I think it is." He knew it was.

"I need you to go through these and select a few cases—"

"No."

"It won't take you that long."

Sacha snorted and crossed his arms over his chest. "It'll take hours, and you know it. That's why you don't want to do it."

"I would, but Gretchen and I have plans with the Sterlings, and I can't cancel again because we canceled last week when the kids were sick and the week before that because Gretchen had a catering gig. And Cherry Sterling is on the Lisieux Academy school board, and if we ever stand a chance of getting the kids in—"

"All right already," Sacha griped, swiping his hand in the air. "Take a breath. My CPR certification has expired."

Paxton strolled across the room and set the books on the desk with a thump before turning to Corrigan with a peculiar smile. "Hi, I'm Paxton."

"Pax, this is Corrigan Ellery," Sacha introduced begrudgingly, shooting his brother a warning stare.

"Nice to meet you," Corrigan replied to which Sacha grunted under his breath.

"Well, I'll let you two get back at it." Paxton hesitated a moment as if he had more to say but left without adding anything.

Looking over his shoulder at the closed door, Corrigan asked, "Are you two twins?"

"No. People always ask that, but I have no idea

why," he deadpanned. He walked in his brother's shadow in more ways than one. "He's adopted."

Corrigan's mouth gaped, and his eyes grew as wide as plates. "No shit?"

Sacha chuckled. "No one ever falls for that. Do you have siblings?" There was a place on the scholarship application for family information, but most of it had been left blank. Sacha assumed that was because Corrigan's coach had completed it and didn't know. However, it also could have been omitted purposefully.

"Two sisters and a brother, all younger."

"Was it hard leaving them?"

Corrigan winced. "It had to happen sometime." He stood abruptly and rubbed his hand across his low fade. "I'm due at the dining hall."

Okay, family may be a touchy subject.

Sacha stood as well. "I can give you a lift."

"No," he rushed, clutching his backpack as if his life depended on it. Several emotions flashed across his face before settling on apprehensive. "Thanks, but Coach worked us out pretty hard." He patted his thighs. "I need to walk to prevent cramping up."

Sacha doubted that was the reason but had nothing to dispute it. "Okay," he replied, squashing the disappointment from his voice. "I'll see you when you're ready to apply for the extension, then?" *Oh, dear heavens. Do I sound desperate?*

"Yeah. Sure." With that, Corrigan bolted for the door and disappeared into the hallway.

Way to scare him off. Sighing, Sacha walked to the desk, sat, and opened one of the books Paxton had left there. *Guess it's me and DoorDash tonight.*

HE'D BEEN READING THROUGH MIND-NUMBING contract cases for Paxton's class when there was a quick rap on the door and one of his mentors and double first cousin, Mace Gardner, appeared in the threshold. Mace was eighteen months younger than Sacha but had been so gifted that he'd graduated high school by age fifteen and completed law school by age twenty-one. Although Mace denied it, Sacha was certain he was a card-carrying member of Mensa.

Sacha's face brightened. "Hey, I didn't know you were in town."

"I was supposed to meet with your father." He unbuttoned his suit jacket, hitched his perfectly pressed trousers, gracefully slid into the chair opposite the desk, and positioned his hands one atop the other upon his lap.

"He and Mother got stuck in Lake Charles unexpectedly. I'm filling in until he returns, but I didn't see your name on the schedule. Anything I can help you with?"

"It was a last-minute add, and probably not." Mace shook his head, his prematurely gray hair barely moving out of place. "He referred a case to me, and something about it isn't sitting right. The client isn't completely forthcoming—although, I truly believe he's innocent—and potential witnesses are nowhere to be found."

"How do you think Father can help?"

"He's known my client's family for ages. I was hoping he could provide me some insight." He crossed his ankle over his knee. "But I don't want to talk about work anymore. How you are?" he asked, relaxing and reverting to his easy Cajun dialect.

"The flu has been more pleasant."

Mace smiled slightly. "Any word on how long Max is planning on keeping you here?"

"Likely until I become as withered as a mummy's dick."

"Glad to hear you're optimistic." His smile

widened, but his eyes grew serious. "I believe most events happen for a reason and that we all have connections to each other and the universe that we don't understand or recognize. It's all a matter of paying attention and asking the right questions when the desirable combination of people comes together."

"Like seven degrees?"

"That and deeper," Mace agreed. "It's not invisible, though, but it requires time, patience, and a keen eye to notice. Eventually, something shakes loose that reveals the bond, and everything begins to make sense. There's this *aha* moment of clarity where the pieces fall into place. Little tidbits become important. People we didn't pay attention to play significant roles. We realize it's one journey but that we took all the side roads instead of the interstate."

"So you're saying this is a blip detour in my career?"

"I'm saying maybe it's more than just your career. Perhaps it's a nudge to reevaluate your entire life. I mean, is law genuinely what you want to do, or is it what you were expected to do?"

Sacha's face contorted. "Not you too."

"What?"

"Paxton and Kian said something similar."

"Then perhaps you should start paying attention."

"But I like practicing law."

"It's all you saw."

Sacha leaned back in his seat and crossed his arms over his chest. "You're one to talk, kettle."

Mace held up his hands in surrender. "I know, I know. I don't have much room here."

"Any room," Sacha corrected.

"Well, I guess not if you're going to be a hardass about it, but I do have a private life. Can you say the same?"

"Yes?" He bit his bottom lip.

"Uh-huh. Exactly." Mace rose. "Will you be at Mitzi's *fais do-do* Saturday?"

"I would attempt skipping, but I think she may have snuck into my bedroom while I was asleep and implanted a tracker beneath my skin."

Mace's laugh billowed in the room. "Leave it to you to think that, but you may be on to something. I'll see you Saturday."

Sacha didn't move for several moments after Mace's departure and reflected on the conversation. Maybe his cousin was right and he was missing the bigger picture.

10

CORRIGAN

"I SHOULDN'T HAVE TO TELL YOU THIS," COACH Massey announced, "but hockey is more than being on the ice. It's mentally preparing yourself and getting in the correct headspace to play. It's training your body to have stamina and endurance and learning your opponents. It includes feeding your body proper nutrition." He glanced at his assistant coach, who nodded in agreement. "If you think hockey is only about making goals, you have a narrow view of the sport overall, and that is not what this is about. You'll be sorely disappointed with such a narrow view. Some of the most dynamic aspects of hockey take place off-ice. Championships are won when teams comprehend and bring all aspects of the game together. Do you hear me?"

A unanimous "Yes, Coach" resounded from the team.

"I expect each of you to do the work—all the work—to earn a place on this team," Coach Massey continued. "You're here now, but that doesn't mean that will be the case once the season starts." He turned to DeSevren. "Have them skate it again."

DeSevren waited until everyone was in place before dropping the puck in the defensive zone. Hansford covered a lot of ice and created a good lane in the middle of the rink. Franley pinched, and Hansford cut hard at his tip, collecting a bank pass. He passed left to Corrigan, who took the shot, and Larousse batted it down with a wide grin. DeSevren blew his whistle.

"Ellery, you have to get your hands away from your body," DeSevren chastised. "Transfer your weight to your inside leg and get that outer leg up so you can put your weight into your low hand and push the puck out in front of you. Then, snap down on the puck. That shot had no power behind it whatsoever. Larousse could have blinked it away."

"You really are lousy," Theriot muttered under his breath as he skated past Corrigan to take Hansford's position to run the play with his line.

"Or maybe Larousse is good."

Theriot parted his lips to rebut but glanced at Larousse, whose eyes narrowed daringly. The captain appeared to reconsider whatever he was going to say and skated in a circle, getting the feel for the ice before stopping at the dot for the drop. He took command of the puck the second the rubber slapped against the ice and barreled straight for the goal with lightning speed. His pass to Cardenas was smooth, and the winger scooped it up effortlessly. Cardenas sent the puck out in front of him as he approached Larousse but then dragged it back with the toe of his stick. Misreading Cardenas's intention, Larousse dove forward, allowing Cardenas to sink the puck over his shoulder and into the rear of the net with flawless execution.

Theriot pumped his fist in the air and shot a smug smirk over his shoulder at Corrigan. "Now that's how you do it."

Although Corrigan wanted to slap the smile off the captain's face, he couldn't be mad that the play had gone as designed. After all, it wasn't Theriot's fault that Corrigan hadn't made the shot, and the only thing he could do was improve his game. But damn if his ego didn't sting… a lot.

He cupped the rear of his neck with his gloved hand and tilted his head back. Squinting at the bright overhead lights, he emitted a groan. He despised being subpar. Inhaling deeply, he attempted to mentally travel to his Zen safe place—not that he'd formally been trained in Zen techniques—and envisioned an optimistic future. *It's only four years.*

"You know, he's skated this drill hundreds of times," Nguyen stated, stopping beside Corrigan. "Don't worry. You'll have plenty of time to get it. It's one of Coach's go-tos. Plus, Ram's line has worked together for a year."

"Yeah, I get that," he replied, focusing on his teammates practicing the drill. But that wasn't the root of the problem. "Hey, Nguyen, where are you from?"

"Natchitoches."

Knack-o-what? Corrigan had no idea how to repeat it, spell it, or where to locate it on a map? "Where's that?"

"It's about a three-hour drive from here."

"Oh. So, have you've always been one of the boys?"

"What do you mean?"

"Fit in. It's not like there's much diversity on the team."

An awareness overtook Nguyen's expression.

"Maybe not this year, but that hasn't always been the case. It has more to do with football."

"How so?"

"If you hadn't noticed, football is all the shit here, and other athletic programs kind of fall by the wayside. A lot of hockey players would rather play for schools that spread the athletic love a little more. Well, that and the rumor that the rink is built atop a voodoo cemetery."

Corrigan's eyes bulged. "Holy shit! Is it?"

"Naw. At least, I don't think so." He shifted his weight. "There was a burial ground somewhere on campus, but the bodies were said to be excavated before any buildings were erected."

"Said to be?"

"Developers can be shady and cut corners. Several years ago, deputies busted a crematorium not too far from here for dumping bodies out back because their incinerator broke. They'd been sending fireplace and incinerated trash ashes to the families. When the hurricane hit, all the corpses washed up from the shallow graves and floated down the city square like a damn Mardi Gras parade. That's how they got caught. Of course, they tried denying it by saying it was an oversight."

Get the eff outta here.

"But most people aren't like that," Nguyen added.

"Let's hope not."

"Anyway, I suspect if the school hadn't relocated the burial grounds, the corpses would have popped through the ice by now. Wouldn't that be something? In the middle of a game and zombie heads springing up like Whack-A-Mole. That would totally violate regulations. Probably a game misconduct."

It took Corrigan a minute to regroup and remember why he'd begun this conversation. "So, I'm not the first Black guy on this team?"

"Far from it. However, you may be the first New Yorker." Nguyen flashed a weak smile. "I know you won't believe me when I say that most people here are good, but the stereotypes from the past overshadow any progress made. Of course, that's not to say that all is perfect or there isn't room for much improvement."

Nguyen's explanation left Corrigan with more questions than answers.

———

WHEN CORRIGAN SIGNED UP FOR HOCKEY CAMP AND Coach Massey said hockey was more than being on the ice, he had no idea it meant this. He flipped open the spiral notebook handed to him by the class instructor and uncapped his highlighter to take notes. Who would have thought he'd have a seminar class about how to interview with reporters? The presenter had demonstrated acceptable standing positions and what to do with one's hands. Each member of the class then had to model each position while answering questions in a mock interview. What's more, they were being graded, and the head coach had expressed that any person not passing would be in jeopardy of not playing.

Nguyen, seated beside Corrigan, leaned over. "A couple years ago, some football players got into a scuffle at a bar, and it made the news. They said some pretty stupid stuff and embarrassed the university. The place has been on lockdown ever since. Goodbye freedom of speech."

Franley, who had his chin resting on his fist with his eyes closed and who Corrigan thought was asleep on his other side, perked up. "Because of those dumbasses, the athletic department got fined. The money earmarked for new seating in the arena got taken away."

Corrigan recalled his shortcut across the football field. "But they're installing new seats in the stadium."

Kavanaugh reared back from the seat in front of them. "Their mistake, our bill. Everyone else always ends up paying for those bozos."

"Coach is determined to make us an exemplary team in every way possible. Get ready to have every aspect of your life micromanaged," Franley added. "If it's not what the coach deems is up to par...." He drew a slash across his neck with his index finger.

Nguyen leaned in closer. "I heard all the coaches and trainers are getting together and forming a prototype media line to promote."

"What's that?" Corrigan asked.

"They're selecting a few players who they think will be the best representation of the team—who play a good game but who are also socially acceptable."

Corrigan's eyes clouded with confusion. "Meaning?"

"Damn, you're dumb," Theriot chimed in from beside Kavanaugh. "They want players who have all the Bs—brains, beauty, breeding, and bank—to parade in front of the world as the college hockey Harvard of the South."

Thoughts began ticking in Corrigan's head—the first being slamming Theriot's face into the desk and sending him to Jesus same-day shipping. However, the second centered on the captain's words. "But if they do that, only put effort in highlighting certain players, agents and scouts will only look at them."

Theriot nodded. "Maybe you're not so dumb."

The thought of smashing Theriot's face reemerged. "The two places I refuse to go to today are back and forth with you."

"I don't see how that's possible," Franley disagreed. "If scouts come to the games, they'll see everyone playing."

"And who do you think will be given the most ice time?" Kavanaugh thumped Franley on the head. "Who do you think the coaches will push for scouts to meet with?"

"Like old Hollywood," Corrigan muttered.

Nguyen scratched his chin. "Huh?"

"Back in the day, movie studio executives would pluck an ordinary person off the street, give them some plastic surgery and dental work, change their name, create a backstory, and boom, they had their new star. Branding."

"Exactly," Kavanaugh agreed. "They write the narrative for everyone to follow. Instead of the audience deciding who should be a star, the studio executives did it for them."

"Now we have committees watching our social

media accounts and scripts written to recite to the press." Theriot swiveled in his chair and faced forward. "Big Brother 1984 has returned."

Corrigan attempted to look indignant, but the conversation disturbed him. He was aware that going pro was equal parts talent and luck. He even knew politics played a role. However, he'd had no clue he'd be starting this soon. Despite all the hype he'd heard surrounding college application, his high school guidance counselor in his sophomore year had conveyed to him a guarded secret regarding the process and saved him a multitude of time and wasted effort. She'd informed him that most colleges only cared about standardized test scores. Persons with perfect grade point averages but low standard test scores were usually denied but not the other way around. Students with high scores and a low GPA frequently found acceptance somewhere, even if it was on probation. It was why standardized test coaching was a multimillion-dollar business and susceptible to buying scores. All the hullabaloo about extracurriculars didn't mean a damn thing unless aiming for an athletic scholarship. And once again, the athletics had been about another set of numbers—the statistics. Stats couldn't be made by bench-warming. Now all that was being flipped on its head with the insertion of another critical factor: aside from numbers, it all boiled down to who a person knew and nepotism.

People grew up with connections, cliques. And outsiders didn't waltz into a clique. They had to receive an invitation. To be invited required being noticed—but not *just* noticed. One had to stand out as being extraordinary, as having that added *oomph*.

"Cuff links."

"What?" both Nguyen and Franley asked in unison.

Corrigan flattened his lips, shook his head, and flipped a page in his notebook.

11

SACHA

Mitzi had plans to fix him up tonight at her dinner party. Sacha could feel it in his bones. In fact, he'd been feeling it all week. The early morning phone call that had woken him from a lovely dream to ensure his presence solidified his suspicion of his sister concocting a scheme. After Xara... Xia... whatever the hell her name was, Sacha didn't have the energy to ride another merry-go-round of disaster, especially not without strong coffee.

He scraped the last grains of coffee from the canister, hoping like hell it would be enough for one cup. After fiddling with the coffeemaker, he sighed. There was no way he could postpone making groceries any longer. Food, he could live without. Coffee, he could maybe survive a couple hours. He didn't need a list because he basically needed everything, but he sat at his breakfast counter where he kept a notepad to make one anyway. So much for sleeping in and basking in a lazy day at home. He hadn't had one of those in a while, and it looked as if that streak would continue into the unforeseeable future.

Before his demotion, his weekends used to be crammed full of meetings with private investigators and mulling over ways to combat prosecutorial evidence. His spirit would be invigorated with how to read a jury and play to their sympathies. Friends called him a workaholic, but his work was also his fun. Now he had a void—or rather a second one. He'd always been able to fill the holes in his personal life with work. But not anymore. Both glared at him with red bulging eyes and a persistence that refused to be ignored.

When he became an attorney, it had given his life a new kind of definition. He'd become important for the first time in his life and stepped outside his family's shadow. Yes, he was still an attorney like the rest of them, but he'd gone into criminal law—fighting for the everyday man and not billion-dollar conglomerate corporations. Okay, so his clients weren't the average Joe Blow on the streets. Millionaires needed defending too. But that wasn't the point. His work mattered. People depended on him, although his parents disagreed on some level.

Sacha's great-grandfather, a probate attorney, opened the practice with his twin brother, who specialized in contracts. After several years of success, they decided to expand the practice into a firm by merging with two other family-run law practices, Calais and Gardner. These included criminal and corporate law. However, the Weymouths through the generations stuck with civil and contract law while the descendants of the other families continued in their families' footsteps. Then Mace, a hybrid of the Weymouth and Gardner families, elected criminal law and gave Sacha the courage to do the same. But perhaps Sacha should have known better than following in his genius cousin's footsteps, because failure was easier to accomplish in criminal law than it was in probate, and Weymouths were not allowed to fail. The thought depressed him nearly as much as the thought of the one lonely egg sitting in his refrigerator.

Since he was up, he decided to check his messages. He skimmed over several texts from his parents—yeah, he was going to have to quit avoiding them—and a few messages from colleagues wanting to play golf. Truth be told, he despised golf and only went because his father had dragged him kicking and screaming. But in actuality, he'd witnessed more business deals than he could count come together by the eighteenth hole. From a business perspective, his playing made sense. He just found the sport to be so incredibly dull. Hit the ball. Walk. Hit the ball again. Walk some more. If you fancy, ride in a one-cylinder wagon with a tarp that could get up to the whomping speed of fourteen miles per hour. And for some really over-the-top excitement when he went buck wild on the course, he could shake the sand out of shoes. Woohoo!

But hockey. People hit pucks. People hit people. People—

A text from an unknown number snagged his attention.

There's no hole to fit it in. How do I link over the button? the message read.

Perplexed, Sacha stared at the message and pondered if it was a wrong number or spam, but not before his mind sank straight into the gutter. The area code didn't register as familiar. None of his clients had his private number, and all his family and friends were programmed into his contact list. The message didn't read as if it came from a business, and he couldn't recall visiting any porn sites. As he decided to swipe Ignore, the phone buzzed in his hand with a second message.

Or do I rip the buttons off?

Could this be someone his mother had passed along his number to for a fix-up? Sacha may not have known who the sender was, but ripping anything didn't sound like a good idea.

That may be a bit rash, he typed in response. **But to be sure, what are we talking about?**

There was a delay before his phone indicated another text. This time, instead of a message, he received a photo of a shirt sleeve and a pair of brassy-colored ball return cuff links that looked one step up from coming out of a drugstore jewelry case.

Huh? He stared at the screen, attempting to figure out the meaning. Who would send him a picture of cuff links and why?

Then it hit him—*Corrigan*—and his belly flipped.

"That's not going to work," he replied at the phone before it dawned on him that he needed to respond via text.

That's a barrel, he typed and clicked Send.

A barrel of what?

A genuine laugh burst from him. Instead of

texting back, he swiped the green phone icon for voice calls. Corrigan answered on the first ring.

"You need a French cuff," Sacha replied as a greeting. "Links can't be used with barrel cuffs."

"Oh."

There was a beat of no response, and Sacha waited for the question he knew would come next. It wasn't rocket science what Corrigan was thinking, but Sacha always enjoyed anticipating a person's next move or statement. It was what he did in law all the time. However, when the silence extended longer than Sacha thought it should, he asked, "What are you doing?"

"Searching French cuffs on Google."

Or you could have asked me since I'm on the phone with you. "I take it you've not been to many formal events."

"I went to prom."

And boom! Sacha was reminded of how young Corrigan was. He could barely remember his senior prom, and honestly, he didn't want to. He'd wanted to ask Frances Borchardt, an outspoken theater student. However, his parents pushed for him to pursue Didi O'Brien, whose conservative beliefs and demure demeanor had been more acceptable in social circles. It had been another disaster in his life, and he'd spent most of the night with Kian and his date.

No wonder Sacha had actively suppressed the memory.

"I wore... barrel cuffs?" Corrigan continued.

Sacha smiled at the phone. "So I also take it you've never worn links before."

"I bought them yesterday. The salesclerk didn't say anything about needing a special shirt. None of the sites I looked at for how to put them on listed anything either."

So I'm the last resort for information. "What's the occasion?"

"I have to take a mandatory interviewing class, and part of the course is mock interviews and... socializing?"

"You don't sound so certain about that last part."

"I don't guess I am." He sighed heavily. "I don't know what I'm doing. I suppose I am one of those naive people who thought hockey was only about hitting a puck around after all. The instructor started talking about meeting boosters and having to speak at fundraisers."

"As much as hockey is a game, on this level, it's a business first. If you continue in it, it's only going to grow bigger. If you think small, you'll be small. The people you're dealing with are looking at the universe and planning how to carve out their portion."

"I'm not sure I'm ready for all this next level."

Something in Corrigan's voice touched Sacha and made him want to help. "I can't assist with the physical stuff, but I do know a little something about prepping witnesses for the stand and media." *Even if they don't follow my advice.* "I was headed into Le Quartier Jardin." He wasn't. The grocery store where he shopped was miles away from Le Quartier Jardin, but he could make a detour. "How about I swing by and take you to The Hub."

"What's that?"

"From what you've told me, it's a place you need to be."

Corrigan

CORRIGAN'S LEGS QUAKED LIKE JELLY COME ALIVE AND clawing its way from the inside out. At 5:00 a.m., Coach DeSevren had awakened the team by running down the dorm hallway banging clash cymbals. Players had little time to toss on clothes and shoes before he ousted them outside for sets of push-ups, squat jumps, and lateral lunges. And since that hadn't stamped the life out of them, he had them sprint to the arena and perform sets of mountain climber burpees, backpedal sprints, and box jumps. Then they'd sprinted back to the dorm for a shower and breakfast. By eight o'clock, Corrigan's every muscle wrenched with pain. However, since it was the weekend, DeSevren said he would go easy on them. Therefore, he had them lift weights until noon, skate drills until two, and gave them the after-noon off until six.

Sacha had agreed—no, insisted—to meet him at the PAC after practice. Corrigan lacked the energy for shopping but doubted he could muster the stamina to drag his tired body up the hills and back to the dorm to pass out. He was thankful for a ride. Plus, he could use Sacha's expertise. A morsel of eye candy to go along with it never hurt either. A naughty tutelage session fantasy popped in his mind as the Mercedes rolled to a stop.

On weekends, most people Corrigan knew looked chill and comfortable. However, Sacha's casual look was put-together and neat in his three-quarter-sleeve navy Mandarin collar polo, bleached sand flat-front chino pants, and navy moccasin driving shoes. A pair of Cartier sunshades with lenses so dark that they completely obscured Sacha's eyes from view perfected his ensemble. Already, Corrigan felt inferior outfitted in worn jeans, a faded graphic T-shirt, and dingy sneakers.

"Thanks for coming, but you didn't have to do this," he said, sliding into the car's cool interior and shutting the door behind him. "I could have figured it out."

Sacha's smile warmed his face. "So you've informed me multiple times. And like I told you, I know I didn't." He waited for Corrigan to buckle his seat belt before he pulled away from the curb.

"Coach only gave us a few hours off."

"That should be enough time. I've already called Truman and made an appointment."

Corrigan's brows shot up. "Appointment? To shop?"

"If you want a custom fit, yes."

"Whoa!" Corrigan raised his hand. "Custom fit sounds like expensive custom price."

"Depends on how you look at it. If you view it as an investment in a few key pieces, it pays for itself."

"Yeah, but paying right now is the issue."

"No worries. I got you."

Jerking back toward the door, Corrigan clenched

his jaw. His chest constricted so tightly that breathing became demanding. "I don't want you paying for me."

His sharp tone had Sacha's head snapping from focusing on the road to him, and Corrigan promptly regretted making the statement.

"I may hold the checkbook, but it's not my money. It's a school expense and therefore covered by your scholarship."

"Clothing?" The skepticism was obvious in his voice.

"If it were a lab coat or safety goggles, would we be having this discussion?"

"That's different."

"Earlier when we spoke on the phone, you said you're required to wear a suit."

"Only on game day."

"And you said the coach suggested you own at minimum three."

"A recommendation, not a mandate. I have one."

"Which means your scholarship will pay for two."

Corrigan expelled a long breath. "I appreciate the offer, but I don't want to waste funds on frivolous items."

They came to a stop at an intersection, and Sacha glanced from the road back to his companion. "I don't think you understand. When this scholarship was created, it was with the intention that the recipient would become a professional athlete—ergo, designed to meet all the needs that encompasses." He turned back to stare out the windshield and kneaded the leather steering wheel firmly. "For recipients falling short of this goal, the idea was that they would be successful in their endeavors and give back by helping create opportunities for future athletes. So you see, this isn't free money. It's a pay-it-forward."

"But—"

"You'll use the suits now for game day. Keep them in good shape and you can use them when you go pro. If you don't, you can wear them for job interviews or on the job. You can wear them at work functions. Think of them as an extension of your uniform. The team provides you with your game and practice uniforms, and the scholarship will provide you with your travel uniform."

Corrigan opened his mouth to speak but then decided against it. He would have never thought of a suit being a uniform. "Sorry."

"No need to apologize. But for the record, not every helping hand is a handout."

Casting his gaze down, he inspected his sneakers.

"I'm used to paying my way is all, never owing anyone. Strings are messy."

"Not when the terms are clearly defined, transparent, and reasonable."

"That rarely happens, even with the smallest of things."

"Why do you believe that?"

Shrugging, Corrigan clasped his hands together. "One time, my aunt from Rhode Island came for a visit. It was her first time visiting the city, and my mom was so excited to have her. She planned for weeks how she would entertain her, starting with us kids drawing a big welcome banner to greet her at the airport. My aunt's reaction to the sign should have been the first indication that the visit wouldn't go smoothly."

"She didn't like the sign?"

"She took one look at it and turned all ruddy. She practically ran past us." He looked over at Sacha, who was scanning a parking lot for a vacant spot. "The plan was to go back to our house, but my aunt wanted to go shopping. My mom tried to explain about the traffic, but my aunt dismissed her and said it wouldn't matter. Long story short, we ended up getting stuck in the evening rush hour."

"That must have sucked."

"It did, but here's the messed-up part. My mom had planned to cook a big dinner, but my aunt complained that she couldn't wait. Every time we passed a restaurant, she whined to stop. My mom is perhaps the most benevolent person you'll ever meet. She didn't have any money because she hadn't planned on staying in the city, and she'd spent a fortune on buying things that would make my aunt comfortable during her visit like new pillows, her favorite soda, fancy soap. But my aunt's whining started turning dark and angry, and she insisted on buying pizza for everyone. My mother acquiesced because my aunt feigned fainting from hunger. Several years later, my mother and aunt had a huge disagreement because my mother had visited my aunt many times, but my aunt always declined to visit us. I'll never forget the look of hurt on my mother's face when my aunt said she refused because on her only visit, she had to buy all of us pizza due to my mother refusing to feed her. It was an outright lie, and she had been spewing that lie to other family members for years without my mother knowing. Then my dad scolded my mom because he said she should have known my aunt would twist the situation."

Sacha pulled into a vacant space and killed the engine. "That's shitty."

It was a shitty story, and Corrigan didn't know why he'd shared it. He'd never conveyed it to anyone. Although it was something that happened to his mother, it had always felt like a family shame. Additionally, speaking the words aloud reminded him how deeply the event affected him. His aunt's words hadn't only hurt his mother, but they had cut him tremendously. He had been a mouth to feed—a reason for his parents' lack of money and his aunt purchasing more than one pizza. He'd been content that day to wait for his mother to prepare her delicious paprika twice-baked chicken but also had been excited to be fed pizza in its stead. When his aunt had turned to him and inquired if he wanted pizza, his face had lit up, and he'd smiled brightly with an eager positive response. He'd eaten the pizza heartily without thought, adding to his aunt's ammunition against his mother. In hindsight, his actions felt like a betrayal to his family, especially toward his mother. And no action he could take would undo it. But no one needed to know about the incident, except obviously he felt Sacha should for some reason.

"My mom has never gotten over it. From that day

forth, none of us kids were allowed to accept anything from anyone, not even after—" He clipped his words.

"After what?"

"Nothing." He turned his focus ahead. "Is this the place?" he asked, despite the store name being displayed in big, bold letters across the front of the building. He'd said more than enough.

12

SACHA

Shopping wasn't something Sacha enjoyed, but it was a skill in his wheelhouse. He staged his clients for juries consistently. He had an eye for what worked and what didn't. However, Corrigan was a special case. A lot of the clothes worked on him if Sacha wished to transform him into a typical college athlete in a suit without an ounce of personality but rather a look-at-me vibe.

"Take it off," Sacha instructed, waving his hand. "You look like you're playing dress-up." He turned to the store clerk. "I'm looking for classic elegance that's not going to age him fifty years."

Corrigan removed the jacket and handed it to a second assistant. His eyes scrutinized Sacha as if unsure. "Coach is trying to bulk me up."

"We'll leave some room," he said, searching through the racks. "Unless baggy is what you're going for—a hip-hop look." He froze and looked up from the clothing, realizing he'd not asked an important question before beginning the search. "What is it that you want for your brand?"

Corrigan shrugged but seemed to consider. "To not look crazy."

"Now there's a word open for interpretation. But what I mean is, what aesthetic expresses you?"

"I don't think I have one. I just put on what's clean. I spend most of my time at practice, so there's no need for more than sweats and a tee."

"Point taken." Sacha leaned against the rack. "Let's look at it from a different perspective. Of the people you know or have seen on television, what styles attract you?"

"I guess sporty that's not all stiff and crunchy."

"Crunchy? Like a taco?"

Corrigan smiled and rested his hands on the back of a nearby chair. "You know. The kind of clothing that makes a lot of noise when you move."

"Ah," he responded, feeling a smidgeon older for not knowing the lingo but happy that Corrigan hadn't pointed it out. "So you're talking stretch cotton or wool."

"I guess." Corrigan hunched his shoulders in a way Sacha found adorable. "Is that bad?"

"Not at all. Not only can cotton be fashionable, but it's also cool and easier to clean. Wool's a might much for this time of year and even in most of the winter, if we're being honest."

"But it's not too… common?"

"It's all about styling—the right fit and color." Sacha moved to the opposite side of the rack to search. "You said sporty. I'm thinking plaid."

"Not just that. I want to look sexy like you."

Sexy? Wait a damn minute.

Sacha's head popped up like a hound catching a scent, his lips curling slightly at the corners before schooling themselves to a more generic expression. His brain wouldn't allow him to graze over a comment like that. Had Corrigan called him sexy? Or had he meant the suit was sexy? Or him in the suit sexy? Was there a difference? *Uh.*

He peered at Corrigan with a thousand rampant thoughts, and the gleam he discovered in the man's eyes shook him. Was Corrigan flirting with him? *Get it right this time.* But that would mean….

He's a hockey player.

Sacha squashed the thought. Instead, he rationalized that Corrigan's comfortability with expressing casual appreciation for someone of the same gender was a generational thing. After all, Corrigan had made the hair comment when Sacha dropped him off at his dorm that could be interpreted as a generalized statement to apply to all men.

Whatever Corrigan had intended, Sacha knew he needed to eradicate the bewildered expression currently on his face that surely would make the situation awkward, especially if he was way off base.

Quit gawking.

"Cornflower blue," Sacha said, finding his voice. "As a color choice." *Really? That's the best you could come up with? Couyon.*

The gleam in Corrigan's eyes dulled, and he stared aimlessly at the pile of disregarded jackets. "I'm not up on color names outside the primary ones."

"I can teach you."

That and a whole lot more.

SUITS, TIES, AND SOCKS PURCHASED, SACHA HAD Corrigan tag along for his adventures in grocery shopping. As he pushed the buggy down the aisle, he couldn't prevent himself from glancing at Corrigan periodically. The tumble of thoughts and emotions occurring within him made him want to fall prostrate and scream into the linoleum. He wouldn't, of course, because there was no imagining what bacterium and fungi customers had tracked across the floor. However, the what-ifs were churning in his intestinal walls. Was he once again being blind to a man seeking his attention? Or was he a victim of an overactive imagination? Did he even want it to be true? Was he attracted to Corrigan?

The last two questions he had answers for. Yes, he fancied Corrigan's interest. If that was wise was another can of worms, wigglers, and whatnots. And most definitely he found Corrigan attractive. He'd been downplaying his dick twitching ever since receiving Corrigan's text message. It wasn't a full-raging hard-on, but it was enough to make its presence known and caused Sacha to walk bowlegged.

He added a bag of rutabagas to his buggy. He had no clue what he'd do with them, but he'd figure it out later.

Corrigan eyed the selection suspiciously.

"You don't like bagas?"

Corrigan's eyes softened when he smiled. "I don't even know what those things are, let alone what they taste like."

"They're a vegetable, and you'll have to make a pass by the house so I can cook them for you."

What the hell? Did I ask him out?

Corrigan's face lit up. "I don't know when I'll be free, but okay."

Holy cannoli. He accepted. What did I just do?

"The coach keeping you busy, huh?"

"I think he's trying to murder us. I've attended some intense training camps before, but none like this."

"Funding."

"What?"

Sacha debated whether he should continue and decided most of the information was already in the public domain, thus he wasn't divulging any confidential university secrets. However, technically, he didn't work for the university and owed them no allegiance.

"More budget cuts are coming down the pike. It's slated to be a 30 percent slash. Massey is trying to spare his program by winning trophies. Championship teams don't get cut. Losing as many players as he did last year, especially Rabalais as netminder, has a lot of sports analysts ranking y'all in the bargain basement this season. But predictions are little more than spitting in the wind—someone is going to get wet, but who? Playoffs are a long, mangled road brimming with potholes from start to finish. Yet they're enough to spook boosters. If the season goes sour, they won't hesitate in seeking a new bench boss."

Astonishment crossed Corrigan's features. "You follow hockey?"

Sacha chuckled. "Don't look so surprised."

"I took you for more of a golf person."

"God, no." Sacha shuddered. "Why would you assume that? You think all attorneys golf?"

"No. You seem like a tremendously busy person who would want a low-key activity to burn off stress in your downtime."

Sacha considered for a moment. "Makes sense." He was about to continue when his cell phone rang. He removed it from his pocket, read the name on the screen, and rolled his eyes. "Yes, I'll be there tonight, Mitzi," he answered without preamble.

"How do you know that's what I called to ask?"

"Because it's what you wanted the first two times you called me today. I'm not going to back out. We'll dance, drink, make merry, and have a blooming good time. I love you, but I have to go. Bye." He disconnected before she responded. "Sorry about that."

"No problem," Corrigan answered, rolling a cantaloupe in his hand with his back to Sacha. "Hot date?"

Hot seat, maybe. He snort-snickered. "Wine party. But knowing Mitzi, I'm sure she's got something *special* planned for me."

"Oh."

Was that disappointment Sacha detected in Corrigan's voice? He sensed something had changed. His gut screamed it, and he didn't like it. *What's happened?* However, he feared that asking would make the tension that had cropped up weirder. Yet he couldn't allow it to persist and decided to ask a noninvasive question.

"How'd you become interested in playing hockey?"

Corrigan replaced the melon on the pile and stared aimlessly around the store with a look of despondency. "It's not an interesting story."

"Try me. I find lots of things interesting."

"My father was a crane operator. When I was eight, he fell off and fractured his spine. It paralyzed him and left him with a severe TBI, virtually wiping his short-term memory. Most of the time, he doesn't recognize us."

"Damn. I'm so sorry."

Corrigan nodded. "It was a long time ago." He attempted to deliver the comment nonchalantly; however, Sacha sensed the pain.

And my nosy ass just had to ask. Guilt raged through him. "Still, that must be difficult to deal with."

"After a while, it becomes part of everyday life. You get used to it. Anyway, at the time, my mom was working as a prop master for a soap opera, but then soap operas lost favor with television audiences. Production relocated her soap to LA to reduce cost, so my mom had to take up odd jobs. One was a private event whodunit company."

"Whodunit?"

"Yeah, like the game Clue or an Agatha Christie novel. My mom decorated the various theme rooms and hid the clues."

"I see."

"A combination of her work hours being insane, inability to afford a babysitter, and my dad not being able to care for me, my mom took me with her. Only I couldn't go on the job with her, so I waited at the ice-skating rink across the street. She'd pop in and have her coworkers check on me during her breaks. Then one day, I was sitting where I usually sat, and one of the new coaches thought I was there for team tryouts but had chickened out. He made me do the drills. When my mom got there and he realized his mistake, he offered to let me join the team for free."

"And it stuck."

"Eventually. My mom didn't want me at home too much. We had moved to a not-so-great neighborhood. Hockey kept me out of the house. Then, when I got a little older and began helping around the house, it—" He stopped abruptly, shoved his hands in his pockets, and walked down the aisle with distress etched on his face.

Don't pry. It's not your business. "Finish what you were going to say." *Way to go, mouth.*

"It was my escape." He hung his head, clearly defeated.

Sacha approached him and placed a hand on his shoulder. "Why is that a bad thing?"

"Because it was selfish to run off when they needed me. I could have taken more shifts busing tables or stayed home to help my siblings with their homework. Instead, I was at practice or on road trips."

The raw emotion in Corrigan's voice ripped through Sacha. "It's not wrong to do something for yourself."

"Yeah, well, I owe it to them to make it to be able

to help out so my sisters and brother won't have to go through what I did."

Don't dare ask. "What was that?" Obviously, his mouth was going to do what his mouth was going to do, brain functioning be damned.

"Getting held back because of the school closing due to insufficient education and its failure to meet state minimal standard regulations. I'll do whatever it takes to move them someplace better."

Ah, that explains why he's a freshman at twenty.

The gravity of Corrigan's statement slapped Sacha square in the face with a reality he hadn't considered. On a subconscious level, he'd always thought jocks to be about partying, getting laid, not interested in grades, and overall reckless individuals. But Corrigan's explanation snuffed out that stereotype. Going to school, playing hockey, and working was a lot of pressure for anyone, especially someone as young as him. He wasn't a typical twenty-year-old. Corrigan's ambition to improve his family's situation garnered Sacha's respect and admiration.

Then another realization struck, and Sacha felt like a wad of chewed tobacco. All his life, he'd been privileged—prestigious private schools' education, a home most would deem a mini-Versailles, and an abled-bodied, healthy family. He'd not wanted for anything, and yet he'd not been as appreciative as he now realized he should have been.

His phone buzzed in his pocket, reminding him of the time. Corrigan had to be back on campus soon. Sacha would be sure not to make him late. Hurrying down the aisle, he plucked what he needed from the shelves and filled his buggy.

13

CORRIGAN

STUPID. CORRIGAN COULD KICK HIMSELF FOR BEING such an optimistic dumbass. When was he going to learn? He dropped his guard for a nanosecond and instantly got dropkicked in the teeth.

For a brief moment in time, he thought Sacha had been flirting with him, or at least receptive to being flirted with. It could have all been in his imagination, but he didn't think so. Sacha hadn't balked when Corrigan called him sexy. In fact, he thought he'd witnessed a shy smile. Or had Sacha been mocking him for being so forward? But later, he thought when Sacha offered to cook for him, it would be a date… kind of. Apparently not. The man had a girlfriend. Of course he did. How could Corrigan expect prime real estate like Sacha to still be on the singles' market? He'd have been gobbled up the first day.

Dumbass.

Besides, what would an ultrasophisticated man like Sacha want with him?

Yet….

Corrigan worked the puck inside-outside, back-hand-forehand in a figure eight through the cone maze Coach Massey had formed on the ice. He needed to focus on the drill and not on Sacha having some hypnotic truth serum effect over him. Each time he was around Sacha, Corrigan found himself spilling his guts. He had to stop doing that. However, he didn't want to. Talking to Sacha was easy, easier than with any other person he'd ever encountered.

Picking up his speed, he rounded the cone for the final time and dashed to the opposite end of the ice to await instructions for the next drill.

"Hey," Nguyen said, elbowing him in the side, "later, a group of us are going to pass a good time at a frat party. You should come. It'll be lit."

Corrigan used the sleeve of his practice jersey to dry the sweat from his face. "You think Coach is going to approve that?"

"Actually, yes. Ticket sales."

"I don't get it."

"Think of the Greek system as the machines in *The Matrix*. Unknown to most, they silently control everything. Members—and there are thousands of them—are expected to perform hours of community service which enhances their visibility, thereby raising their public profile both on campus and in the community. Members are also expected to support other members, which equates to butts in seats at games. But it's not solely members in their organization but other Greek houses as well. Basically, it's grassroots door-to-door advertising."

"Damn, does everything has an angle?"

"What can I say? It's college athletics, and we compete on every level. So, are you in?"

Corrigan parted his lips to refuse but remembered the conditions of his scholarship as well as the conversation he'd had with his teammates in the interview seminar. Already dog-tired, he didn't know how he'd get through a party of any sort. However, he could use it as an excuse to text Sacha again and ask him for advice. But how desperate and cringy would that be? Sacha was preparing for a date, for Pete's sake. He wouldn't want to be bothered. *Leave him alone.* Then again, he did tell Corrigan he could call him anytime.

"Sure, if you're certain Coach will be okay with it."

"Trust, he'll have spies there."

Corrigan wanted to ask who the spies were, but the whistle blew for the next drill. Taking his position at the line, he handled his stick to the front and then to the side before pulling back and sliding the puck through his feet. Although he'd practiced this drill with his old team, he struggled with how Coach Massey had modified it with a direction transition after every pull-through, and his thoughts lingering on Sacha didn't help his coordination.

Spinning for the direction change, Corrigan momentarily lost sight of his puck in his blind spot before it came back into view. He extended his stick and dragged it toward him but immediately realized it wasn't his puck. The freakish sequence of events that followed was anyone's guess, but Corrigan's stick lodged in the top of the captain's boot.

Plunk!

"Yow!" Theriot yelled, crashing to the ice with a thud. He spun on his belly across the ice while Corrigan's stick helicoptered through the air and landed in the bleachers.

The shrill of DeSevren's whistle pierced through the arena. For a split second, the entire team stood slack-jawed and wide-eyed before bursting into hysterics.

"What in tarnation was that?" DeSevren questioned, scratching the bristles on his jaw.

"You did that on purpose," Theriot accused, scrambling to his feet, his face scarlet.

It would have been hilarious had it been, but Corrigan couldn't have orchestrated that masterful debacle had he tried.

He shrugged. "Umm… karma?"

"Well, whatever it was, don't do it again," DeSevren ordered.

Shaking his head, Coach Massey scowled with an expression somewhere between disgust and disbelief. "I think they've had enough," he said to his assistant. "Wrap 'em up." He shook his head again and skated off the ice.

"Okay, Minotaurs, let's bring it in for the chant."

Well, hell, if Corrigan knew that was how to end practice, he would have aimed to do it hours ago.

As he crossed the Gamma fraternity house threshold, the scents of stale cigarettes, booze, and tawdry perfume descended on him. Following his teammates, he hedged from the entry hallway through the dense crowd to a large gathering room with a vaulted ceiling, floor-to-ceiling windows, and a stone fireplace. For a place that housed dozens, the space felt impersonal with its sleek and modern design but still held a marked male influence. It wasn't what he'd imagined the inside of a frat house to look like, but it wasn't what he hadn't imagined either. From the exterior, the mansion resembled a relic of *Gone with the Wind*—as did all the other fraternities on Fraternity Row, as well as the sorority houses on Sorority Row—but the interior was in stark contrast. The jitteriness of uncertainty Corrigan had been feeling intensified.

He'd expected to witness a sloppy drunk fest, and within thirty seconds, his expectations had been met. Gathered in clumps, cliques communicated with grand gestures and exaggerated expressions while hugging each other to remain upright. Initially, he'd thought no fraternity members were present at their own party because he couldn't distinguish members from nonmembers. However, he later learned that chapter rules dictated that no member could be seen—or perceived as being—intoxicated while representing the organization. Thus, members were not allowed to wear their letters anywhere alcohol was served. Although small, it was another detail the movies Corrigan had seen featuring Greek life had gotten wrong but he'd assumed was true.

K-pop spilled from a sound system that pumped music throughout the house, but it was mostly inaudible due to uproarious chatter and boisterous laughter. It wasn't his favorite type of music, but he could get into it.

"Let's grab some brews," Nguyen suggested.

While downing a cold one sounded ideal to calm his nerves, Corrigan remembered Coach Massey's spies. Getting busted for underage drinking the first week wouldn't sit well with anyone and could derail all his plans. Besides, he didn't trust any of his present company enough not to have his wits about him at all times.

"I'll stick with soda," he replied.

"Soda, ha-ha," Kavanaugh called over his shoulder, heading to a makeshift bar. "Pussy."

Larousse started to follow Kavanaugh but was highjacked by a raven-haired beauty who stepped in his path and superciliously folded her arms across her voluptuous bosom. "And where do you think you're going?"

Larousse wiggled his brows. "Obviously with you

and any place you take me." He swung his arm around her shoulders. "Lead the way."

With a giggle, the coed clamped her hand over his, and the two disappeared into the crowd.

"Yo, Bo," called a thin guy with hair that looked stiff with product. "How's it going, man?"

"Hoyt," Nguyen greeted in return with a fist bump. "It's all good."

"I see you got paroled from the ice prison." Hoyt laughed. "I didn't expect to see you until spring. Word in these streets is y'all not getting any conjugal visits until after playoffs—if you make playoffs."

"We will."

"Yeah? Team any good? Y'all lost a lot of good players last season."

"And gained some good ones." Nguyen turned to Corrigan. "Hoyt, meet Corrigan Ellery, one of our new wingers. Corrigan, this is Hoyt Lemelle, rabble-rouser and vice president of this here shanty."

Hoyt's hooded eyes appeared to conceal a smile as he extended his hand to shake. "I haven't seen you around campus."

"It's the first flipping week," Nguyen replied.

Corrigan shook Hoyt's hand. "As you said, practice keeps us busy."

"Well, I'll be waiting to see if it pays off. I'm going

to be pissed if I drop a couple hundreds on you guys and you turn out to be shit."

A surge of pride struck Corrigan. "Your money will be well invested."

"Ah, big talk." Hoyt nodded. "Confidence. I like that. I like big returns better. I'm in finance. What's your major?"

"Gen—" He caught himself. "Architecture."

"Impressive." Hoyt grinned, placed his hand on his own shoulder, and tapped his fingers.

"Oh, brother," Nguyen mumbled beneath his breath.

"Difficult major. You must be super smart to tackle it and hockey."

"I don't know about smart, but I intend to work hard at both," Corrigan replied. "I'm used to juggling hockey with other things."

A guy who Hoyt introduced as Alton joined them. "Alton's majoring in environmental design. He can tell you a lot about the department."

Corrigan spent the next several moments engaged in conversation with both Hoyt and Alton before a guy named Bullard joined them and Hoyt disappeared. At some point, Alton left, too, and Corrigan chatted with a guy named Omari, and finally with a guy nicknamed Pelahatchie. Other than them each having an odd habit of tapping their shoulders, Corrigan thought they all seemed pretty chill.

After Pelahatchie wandered back into the crowd, Corrigan realized Nguyen was gone as well. He searched the room and didn't see any of his teammates. He deduced that they'd probably ditched him to return to the dorms, leaving him to navigate his way back in the dark, which wouldn't be fun.

As he made his way toward the front door, an inebriated coed crashed into him. Her ankle twisted awkwardly in her stiletto, and Corrigan caught her before she slammed to the floor. Her drink splashed in his face as she puked down the side of his leg.

"Shit fire!" Corrigan yelled, gagging and struggling to not see his meal again as he felt the puke soaking through his pants. The force of her falling body pushed him back, and he collided with a brawny guy who had him outmatched by weight and height.

"Watch it," the guy growled.

"Sorry, man. It was an accident."

The guy's stony gaze sharpened and then narrowed with a flash of dark emotion, his displeasure displaying in the taut restraint of his lips. His burly chest bowed outward as the robust muscles in his biceps flexed beneath his gabardine Henley with the sleeves hoisted up to his elbows. "Stupid bitch," he added, shoving Corrigan in the shoulder as the group he was with turned their attention to Corrigan as well.

"Don't put your hands on me," Corrigan stated firmly but maintained his composure.

"Or what, bitch boy?"

"Or we kick your ass," a voice behind Corrigan responded.

I know that voice. He turned to find Theriot standing behind him, the lines in his face hard and ready for battle. *Wait. Theriot's my avenging angel? What the fuck?*

"Sit your punk ass down," the guy spat, stepping forward as if he was going to do something.

Theriot stepped up to meet him. "Why don't you backstroke to the deepest pit of your ratchet, dilapidated lair and take all your kowtowing minions with you? Swerve, bitch."

The guy's jaw tightened, and he attempted to push past Corrigan. However, Corrigan pressed his palm against the guy's chest, holding him in place. "I wouldn't."

"Oh, you wouldn't?" the guy mocked in an insidious whisper, his lips curling back like a wolf baring its fangs, and slapped Corrigan's hand away. "I'll snatch your trachea out of your throat." He faked to turn but instead threw a sucker punch at Corrigan and landed a snap jab to Corrigan's rib cage, knocking the breath out of him. While doubled over, the guy snatched Corrigan's hair to pull him upright. Corrigan retaliated with a knee to the crotch, and the big guy went down to his knees.

As a second guy jumped in, Theriot lunged forward, knocking them all backward and into furniture. Bodies scattered in all directions, and more joined the skirmish. Corrigan wasn't sure who he was fighting, but he connected his fist to the flesh of anyone he didn't recognize. *Fucking insane.*

Within minutes, someone yelled that campus police were on the way, and Corrigan knew this was not a place he needed to be found. It was all about to hit the fan.

Nguyen grabbed him by the collar. "Come on. We have to get out of here."

Corrigan didn't argue and followed Nguyen outside to where Kavanaugh, Theriot, and Larousse were gathered on the porch.

"Okay, everyone knows the drill," Theriot commanded.

"What's the drill?" Corrigan asked as everyone else nodded.

Theriot released a frustrated breath. "Split up and get an alibi, moron."

"What the hell is your deal?" Corrigan snapped. "Seconds ago, you were ride-or-die, and now you've reverted to complete asshole."

Theriot's lips spread in what Corrigan thought might almost be amusement. "I can say things like that to you. He can't."

"That's all kinds of fucked-up."

"A discussion for a later time," Larousse stated. "Right now, we gotta disappear."

"Right," Nguyen agreed. "See you guys back at curfew."

And just like that, within seconds his teammates had dashed in opposite directions.

In the distance, he heard the campus police sirens. He hurried down the steps and turned in the direction opposite the sirens. Unsure of where to head, he hurried down Fraternity Row toward where he thought he'd seen a path leading to the main campus. However, he soon found himself in the backyard of another fraternity house where there was a party in full swing. In the center of the yard, a long table was covered with newspaper. Atop the newspaper was a heap of boiled potatoes, peeled onions, short corn on the cob, and crawfish.

"Oh, dude, what happened?" a guy dressed in a plain T-shirt with the sleeves folded, Levi's, snake-skin cowboy boots, and a pinched front cowboy hat asked. He gestured toward Corrigan's soiled pants.

"Some girl—"

The guy raised his hand. "Say no more. Come inside, and we'll get you cleaned up. I'm Leo, by the way."

"Corrigan."

"Yeah, I know. I recognized you from your recruiting photo in the *Minotaur Advocate*, the school newspaper," He opened a patio door to a laundry room. "Think you'll be starting?"

"That's up to Coach."

"But he has favorites, right? Players who he's paying close attention to during practice?"

Yes, but I'm not telling you. "He looks at all of us and at whose style best complements the others on the ice with him."

The answer seemed to satisfy Leo, and he handed Corrigan a towel and a spray bottle. "Emergency stash," he explained. "It's vinegar and water. You'll smell like Italian salad dressing for the rest of the night, but it'll take out the stain and cover the stench."

"Thanks," Corrigan said, accepting the items. "I take it this has happened before."

Leo grinned. "A time or two."

They continued to chat while Corrigan cleaned himself up, and then the two returned to the backyard. At Leo's insistence, Corrigan prepared himself a plate of food and chitchatted about hockey, majors, and hobbies with Leo and a few of his friends who were making their way through the party. Strangely, Leo had the same habit as the Gamma house guys of tapping his shoulder.

By the time Corrigan decided to return to the dorm, he'd found his night hadn't been as dreadful as he'd expected and that most people he'd met had behaved decently.

14

SACHA

I'M GROWN, SACHA REMINDED HIMSELF. HE'D BEEN AN adult and independent for quite some time. So why was he cowering away in a corner of a dark room in his sister's house? Good thing he wasn't afraid of the dark.

Was his life really this pathetic?

He sipped his wine and looked out the large window over the lake. It was a beautiful view. But he had a beautiful view from his home too. So why didn't he go home? Well, he knew why. While he'd been able to sneak off through the house, Mitzi had stationed her cronies at the doors. Okay, they were service workers for hat check and valet, but they diligently reported all comings and goings of guests to his sister. If he dared try to escape, they'd have the bat signal or the dark mark in the sky before he fastened his seat belt. But as long as she knew he was looming somewhere, he was safe—well, safe enough. She would assume he was engaged in some mindless conversation with any one of the strings of women she'd invited on his behalf and had practically betrothed to him.

Normally he would entertain the thought of playing the game and dancing the waltz—do the "small talk and exchange digits" thing. However, tonight, he couldn't stomach pretending. After a few minutes of schmoozing through the guests, he knew no one there piqued his interest, and his mind kept drifting to earlier in the afternoon with Corrigan and how a comfort had seated itself in him during their time together. He'd not felt compelled to carefully construct his statements to avoid disclosing his private thoughts. Corrigan would listen without judgment. Sacha felt it.

Besides, if Paxton, Kian, and Mace were correct, Sacha owed it to himself to be authentic. And if that meant exploring his sexuality, then so be it. Maybe he was one of those people who could get turned on by the fantasy but chicken out when it came to the follow-through. Or maybe he was a person who wanted what he couldn't have. Was Corrigan even available to him? Was he attracted to Corrigan because unavailable people were safe and would give him an excuse not to answer the questions Paxton had raised?

Shit. He was driving himself crazy. At least if he still had criminal law in his life, he would have a distraction.

Closing his eyes, he leaned against the wall.

A courtroom would allow him to remain in his comfort zone and within the expectations of others. The only problem with remaining in his comfort zone was that a part of him was itching to know the unexplored.

He couldn't shake the thoughts of Corrigan from his mind.

In typical Sacha fashion, he'd created a mental list of all the cons of being with Corrigan. Most were relevantly weak and fear based. The only strong, legit concern—well, there were two, assuming he was indeed gay—was the age gap. How much would they have in common? Wouldn't Corrigan want to have a full college experience? Play the field? Swing from chandeliers? Streak buck naked across the stadium? Okay, maybe not the last one, but Sacha wouldn't judge.

He had dated—a lot. He was tired of the scene

and desired something steady, and this led directly to his second legit concern. Corrigan was so young. He wouldn't want to be tied down and settled. If Sacha allowed himself to fall for him, he very well could end up nursing a broken heart, which would probably be worse than being alone. Again, this assumed that Corrigan was both interested and gay.

Sacha knew investigators and had an entire catalog of them in his contacts. He could always give one a call and have them snoop into Corrigan's private life. However, that felt like a violation—borderline cringy slash stalkerish—especially when Sacha hadn't bothered (aka manned up) to ask Corrigan about it. How was he to figure it out? He considered for another moment and decided, *Screw it.* He slipped his phone from his pocket and typed a text.

Hope you made it to practice on time. I know we cut it short, and it has me worried. I wouldn't want to be the reason you're skating laps or anything. Lies. All lies. Sacha had dropped Corrigan off at the PAC for practice with time to spare. But since this was the angle he was taking, he needed it to sound convincing. **I also didn't want to text too soon and interrupt.** *Or appear desperate*—which he probably did.

All good came the reply minutes later.

That's it? That's all he's going to give me? Disappointment swept over Sacha. He didn't know why he'd expected that to open a dialogue, but he had. He sucked at flirting.

Great. I'll be able to sleep better knowing.

He was about to slide his phone into his pocket when it vibrated again.

You're in bed? Sounds cozy.

Ah! There was his opening. Sacha debated how to proceed and decided to go all in. **It would be if I were and weren't alone.** *Let's see what he does with that.*

What happened to your wine date?

I'm sipping a glass while attempting to construct a plausible exit strategy. My fallback used to be having to meet a client at the jailhouse for an interrogation. It takes more effort to fabricate a contract emergency.

I'll call you if they haul me down to the campus police station.

Sacha's brows bunched, and concern crept into his eyes. **Why would you be taken there?**

Fraternity brawl.

You're joking, right?

Unfortunately, I have the upchuck on my pants as evidence.

Should I even ask? **What happened?** *I guess so.*

A drunk chick must have thought her body was on fire and decided to stop, drop, and roll right into me. Are you certain the nonnegotiable is nonnegotiable?

Irrefutably, but if you would like to discuss it, we can. I can even arrange an emergency consult tonight.

Wow. You must be desperate to get out of where you are.

Yep. Sacha scowled. Although true, he wanted to retain some form of dignity. However, he was willing to make the sacrifice if it meant spending the rest of the evening with Corrigan.

Wait. Did he honestly feel that way? He considered the thought and came to the conclusion that he did.

All in, right?

I enjoy your company.

He held his breath as he awaited the response. *Was that too much? Too weird? Inappropriate?* Why was he worried about being inappropriate when he'd already referenced sleeping alone? A case—a weak one, granted—could be argued for sexual harassment. Well, whatever it was, it was too late because he'd already hit Send. *Kee-yaw!*

Admit it. You like me because I don't mind getting cans from the bottom shelves at the grocery store so you don't have to stoop low.

Sacha laughed aloud. *That's not the reason.* It wasn't the cans on the bottom shelves that he'd wanted. Rather, he enjoyed the scenery—Corrigan bent over with his ass—

"There you are," Mitzi huffed, entering the room. "I've been looking for you for half an hour."

Sacha jumped, startled. *Ah, crackers! Busted.* He'd swear his sister was part bloodhound.

His smile faded as he turned to face Mitzi. "I haven't been gone that long."

"Right. It's been longer, but that's when I missed you."

"I needed air."

"You promised."

"Yes, to come, and I'm here, aren't I?"

"You said you'd try."

He held up his phone. "I have—"

"No, don't you dare say you have to leave. Harvey took over your caseload."

"Fine." Sacha slipped his phone into his pants and groaned. The thought of returning to the others brought bile to the base of his throat. He took a step and then stopped. Suddenly, he felt like a fraud lying to his sister. "No, it's not fine." Reaching for Mitzi's elbow, he pulled her toward him. "Mitz, I think I'm gay."

"What?" Her eyes glossed with a glaze Sacha couldn't identify, and her energetic demeanor crumbled.

He braced himself for a reaction of mortification, disgust, and condemnation to hell—a typical response from his family when something occurred outside of what was deemed respectable. After all, they were Weymouths, the epitome of tradition and conservatism. Articulating the words had made his soul quake, and he wasn't sure he didn't regret his spontaneous confession. Was he ready for this? Losing the affection of his sister would slice deep, especially since he still had so many questions for himself.

For what seemed like an eternity but couldn't have been longer than a few seconds, a deafening silence filled the room. "Well, that changes things," she finally murmured, her lips puckering the way they always did when she was deep in thought. "You should have said something sooner so I could have planned better. I may have time to change the seating chart. George's cousin is here, and I think he's gay. Rumor has it that Hunter is bi, but it's nothing solid." She scrunched her nose. "I don't think you'd want to get involved with him, though. He harbors enough pettiness to choke a mean girl."

"Seriously? I come out to you, and all you have to say is that I screwed up your seating arrangements?"

"What do you want me to do? I could leave it as is if you prefer, but how are you going to chat comfortably with these men if you're at the opposite end of the table?"

Speechless, he studied his sister's determined glare. "You're unbelievable."

"Why? Because I want you to be happy?"

"Who says I'm not happy?"

Mitzi crossed her arms, her tone nonchalant and assessing. "You're alone. Even misery doesn't always dine alone."

"I'm *single*. There's a difference. Lots of people are single."

"Lots of people like anchovies too."

He paused, his words once again lost. "That makes no sense as a rebuttal."

"You want to know what makes no sense?" Her jaw clenched in a stubborn line. "That you would wait this long to share this with me. I'm your sister."

"I'm just now figuring it out myself, so it would be appreciated if you didn't go blaring it to the nation yet."

Mitzi's eyes glinted with sadness as if she might cry. "I don't want you keeping secrets from me."

His face softened as he drew her to him in an embrace. "I would never."

"Trevor Lampley recently broke up with his boyfriend," she mumbled into his chest.

And while he wouldn't keep secrets from her, that didn't mean she wouldn't continue to meddle in his life. He was certain, the minute they left the room, she'd begin pimping him out to any man in the vicinity with a dubious sexual reputation.

Poo-yi.

15

CORRIGAN

IF CORRIGAN HAD LEARNED ANYTHING DURING THE past week, it was that Coach Massey indeed had spies and plenty of them. After returning to the dorm for curfew on Saturday, he and the rest of the team had been met in the lobby by the assistant coach, who spent ten minutes chewing them out and another thirty minutes having the team perform push-ups and squats as punishment for the frat house scrimmage. But the discipline hadn't stopped there. Coach Massey had lengthened practices and doubled down on drills to the point that Corrigan's muscles were too sore to be sore. The situation had become so dire that even Theriot forgot to be an asshole on most days.

Likely the practices violated NCAA regulations,

but who paid attention to the rules during the off-season? Besides, conditioning and weight lifting weren't technically considered *practice*, which gave Coach Massey a vast loophole, not to mention when workouts were labeled as *student-led* and, thus, exempt from being monitored. The logistics of the rights and wrongs of the hockey program being run could be argued to the moon and back. However, nothing would be done because the system was too well oiled. The people who counted knew the precise language to use and how to skirt the lines of acceptability. So this was the price Corrigan would pay.

When his body wasn't being physically pushed to its limits, his mind was being challenged in class-room seminars on interviewing, nutrition, tactical sessions, and game mentality preparation. With both his body and mind drained, all he wanted was to crash, decompress, and relax. If he could find a reason to smile or laugh a little, even better. So, when Coach Massey cut them loose at six o'clock on Friday and said they could have Saturday off with no curfew to attend the dedication of the new Student Aquatic Center, Corrigan was elated. That was until Nguyen charged into the dorm room Corrigan shared with Marshall Girid, a rookie defenseman from Livonia, Louisiana, without knocking.

Girid never said much to anyone; thus, the room was mostly quiet—*mostly* being the opportune word. When awake, Girid usually wore noise-canceling headphones while he streamed or listened to music. But when asleep, he snored like a tractor, leaving Corrigan with more restless nights than not. Having a free Friday evening for Corrigan translated to being able to catch some z's before Girid crawled under the sheets and cranked the bulldozer. His evening had been looking better when Girid hadn't returned from practice. But now Nguyen was looming in the middle of his room with a forlorn expression.

"Problem?" Corrigan asked, his hands crossed behind his head on his pillow.

"It will be for you if you don't get out that bed."

Corrigan's brow arched. "And why is that?"

"A little birdie told me Coach has planned another room raid, and anyone found here is going to catch it all weekend."

"But he gave us time off."

"A farce for us to let our guards down. He's coming, and he's coming hard. I hear it's a trip out into the woods to a deserted Army Reserve obstacle course. I suggest you pack a bag and find a place to lie low for the next thirty-six hours unless you want to play G.I. Joe."

Corrigan sat upright, concern etched on his face. "I guess I can get a cheap hotel room."

Nguyen shook his head and snorted. "That's the first place he'll look. You don't think he has goonies stashed at the front desks who will call to snitch the instant you check in?"

"Where is everyone else going?"

"Different places. Friends. The ones who live nearby are rolling home."

"What about you?"

"I'm busting a nut at this chick I met's studio apartment. She's like six feet tall with triple Ds. I figure it'll take twenty-four hours to satisfy her and another twelve for me to recover." He chuckled, wiggling his eyebrow. "I thought I'd give you a heads-up before heading out. If you're going to go, you better move fast. Roundup begins in about twenty minutes."

"Twenty? Shit!" Corrigan sprang from his bed and snatched his athletic bag from a chair.

As Nguyen turned to leave, he paused by Corrigan's desk and lifted several colorful index card-size envelopes. "What's all this?"

Corrigan shrugged as he opened drawers and crammed clothes into his bag. "They were taped to the door when I returned."

Nguyen flipped the envelopes in his hands. "Looks like someone's being recruited."

"What?"

"These are dirty invites. Frats pass them out to people they're interested in recruiting." He opened one of the envelopes and pulled the card from inside. "Chi Delta Upsilon. Interesting. I didn't know you were pledging."

Corrigan shook his head. "I'm not. I mean… I completed an intake application, but I had to as a condition of my scholarship. And what do you mean by dirty?"

"Technically, they're not supposed to make contact with any PNMs until recruitment officially begins."

"PNMs?"

"Potential new members. It's supposed to keep recruiting fair by balancing bids because some houses are more popular than others. But when a house finds a person they like, they stoop to dirty recruiting by sending out invites before the other houses have an opportunity to meet the PNM." He waved the envelopes. "Seems like you've caught a couple eyes."

"I don't know how. I've only been to that one fraternity...well, aside from when I accidentally walked up the drive of another. A guy there let me get cleaned up."

"So you cleaned up and left?"

"I got some food."

"Mm-hm. Didn't talk to anyone?"

Corrigan rummaged through a crate beside his bed where he stored his hygiene products. "A couple guys as they stopped for a few minutes on their way to the food table."

"Let me guess. They mysteriously appeared after the person you were talking to developed an itch on his cheek or chin that had to be scratched."

Looking up from the crate, Corrigan frowned. "What?"

"You didn't notice any of them do anything weird?"

"No. Well...." He reflected for a moment. "Except they tapped their shoulders a lot."

Nguyen glanced down and shook his head. "You're so naive. That's code for another member to come in to help scope PNMs." He tossed the envelopes back on the desk. "You're on their radar.

Anyways, I've got to boogie if I want to avoid Coach's henchmen. You'd better do the same."

"On it," Corrigan replied, haphazardly flinging toiletries in his bag. His mind whirled as he scanned the room for any other items he may need while in hiding.

Dear God, this is like some black ops thing.

Seeing nothing else necessary, he stuffed his feet into his shoes, grabbed his wallet, and rushed out of his room and down the side stairs, where a few of his teammates scurried with apparently the same intentions. Once outside with no plan of where to go, he picked a random direction and began speed walking.

AT SOME POINT DURING CORRIGAN'S WALK, HE'D decided to head to the library. Who would think to look for a jock in a library, right? He figured it wasn't the safest place to hide since it was bound to have spies, but it also had plenty of dark cubbyholes and would get him out of the open.

"Where's the fire?"

Startled, Corrigan jerked his head in the direction of the voice. Between two vehicles in a parking area, Sacha was leaning against an SUV with a pretty —*exceptionally pretty*—woman in a stylish suit beside him.

"Oh, hey," Corrigan responded, coming to a halt and taking a second to find his voice. His eyes floated up the beauty, from her long legs crossed in front of her to her cinched waist accented by a designer belt to her draped blouse covering a generous bosom to her oval face with high cheekbones and sculpted nose. Beautiful and exactly what he imagined would be Sacha's type. Something about her looked familiar, yet Corrigan knew he didn't know her. "All around, apparently."

"That sounds cryptically alarming."

"I don't mean to be. It's just—" He cut his sentence short and glanced nervously over his shoulder with his heart thumping against his rib cage as a convertible with the top down sped past. Not recognizing any of the passengers, Corrigan sighed a breath of relief before tensing again. Coach's spies could be anyone, including students in a ragtop.

To some, this would appear as a petty overreaction. Sure, his situation wasn't on the same level as being hunted by international terrorists or drug lords, but he had to remind himself that this was hockey culture. While he'd never experienced anything to this level on his previous team, he'd heard stories and had a comprehensive under-standing of how it worked. Much like a military hell week, some athletic programs were designed to test endurance by physically and mentally taxing players to the edge to eradicate the *weak*. The merit of that philosophy could be debated, but the fact remained that those serious about going pro accepted the chal-lenge without pushback or questions. Those who failed to comply with the draconian training condi-tions and code of silence didn't advance. All he'd experienced the past week was nothing compared to what he imagined the coach had planned for the weekend. Being hidden away in secluded woods created an ideal no-holds-barred condition. While whistleblowing might be an option if someone was willing to listen, no player ever wanted to be labeled as the one who distracted focus from the team's goal of winning games. And that was exactly what Coach Massey would ticket this weekend as.

"I have to go," Corrigan finally replied.

"Wait," Sacha called after him. Turning to his companion, he pecked her on the cheek and informed her that they would talk later. He jogged across the parking lot to catch up to Corrigan, whose long strides had taken him several paces in a few seconds. "Wait," he requested again, clutching Corrigan's elbow. "What's going on?"

Corrigan came to a full stop at the firm grip. "I need to get to the library."

"Sure. I'll give you a ride."

"No—"

"My car is right over there." He jerked his head toward the building. At Corrigan's hesitation, he added, "I have to pass there on my way home."

Corrigan bit his bottom lip as another car motored down the street, and his anxiety rose another notch. He was certain—well, mostly—that a van wouldn't roll up beside him, have people dressed as ninjas jump out, shove a sack over his head, and drag him inside. However, if he were located and refused to go, he couldn't imagine good results. His body needed the rest.

"Thanks."

The two walked to Sacha's car and climbed inside. Initially, neither spoke as they began the short drive to the campus library. However, Sacha broke the silence.

"You seem a bit on edge."

"Yeah, I guess I am." Corrigan attempted a smile but failed. "I'll settle down once I get to the library."

"Is there some special event happening?"

"No. I'm going to hang out for a while."

"In the library?" Sacha's brows bunched.

"I get it. Jock and library equal an oxymoron."

"Not at all, but it's Friday. The library closed half an hour ago."

"Shit!" *Think.* He considered places to go. *The mall? Is that too obvious? Maybe the movie theater where it's dark.*

"You seem a bit scattered. What's going on?"

"I need a place to hide for a few days."

"Why? Are you in trouble?"

"Not the way you think." Quickly, he rambled through his dilemma.

"Well, that's simple enough. Come to my place."

The hideaway was perfect, but… "No, I couldn't."

"Why not? No one will look for you there. My house is safe. I have haint paint and everything."

"What paint?"

"It keeps the Lutin at bay. Trust, I'm too old to have spirits running amuck in my attic, especially if they aren't paying rent or doing laundry. Do you have any idea what exorcisms cost?"

Exo…? What the…? Gah! Let it go. Do not fall down this rabbit hole.

"Besides," Sacha continued, "even if someone did

come searching, they wouldn't make it past gate security. So, why not stay?"

Because being around you causes me to spring a boner? No, Corrigan definitely couldn't answer with the truth, but he could think of no other excuse. So, against the better judgment of his raging libido, he agreed.

16

SACHA

Why was Sacha nervous? He'd had houseguests before, although none had ever stayed overnight. He valued his privacy, but mostly, a situation had never arisen that a friend or colleague had needed to crash at his place. If they'd had problems with their significant others or spouses, they rented a hotel room or returned to their condos where they'd never terminated the leases. And women... well, that was an entirely different story. Awkward morning-afters had never been his jam. He preferred to do his business—preferably not in his house—and go.

Again, he questioned if his actions were ethical. Technically, Corrigan wasn't his client, and neither was ULSA. But would the bar and ethics committee see it that way? Would his legal peers? Would this smear the Weymouth name... further? Sacha was already in deep enough shit with his father without adding to it. Pissing him off even more wouldn't help him get back to practicing defense law again.

Sacha selected a bottle of wine from the cabinet in his kitchen but then remembered Corrigan was underage. Deciding sweet tea would be a better option to go with their meal of apricot orange glaze butter steak, zucchini fries, and roasted chickpea salad, he returned the bottle. Yes, he was going out of his way to impress Corrigan with his cooking skills.

Okay, if he was forced to come clean about the meal, the food had been frozen leftovers from Mitzi's party. The benefit of being the single sibling was that at the end of any family event, his family ensured he was loaded with leftovers as if he would starve without them. It was a phenomenon he didn't understand, but certainly not one he'd complain about. And unless Corrigan insisted on knowing, not one Sacha felt compelled to confess. After all, he'd warmed and plated it. That counted for something, right? Besides, it wasn't as if he'd had advanced notice to plan a proper... what? Did this count as a date? Damn. Why did he feel so incognizant and inept?

He strolled into the living room where he'd left Corrigan to have some privacy as he video-chatted with his mother, who'd called. He found Corrigan seated on the sofa, fumbling through his athletic bag and muttering.

"Everything okay?"

"Yeah. My phone died, and I can't find my charger. I threw everything in so fast. I think I grabbed it, but I'm not sure."

"I probably have one that fits." Sacha walked to the wall shelving unit and opened a drawer. He returned to Corrigan with a storage case of a neatly twined assortment of extension cables, port heads, and power plugs.

"Whoa. Are there any adapters left at Best Buy?"

"I use a lot of different devices."

"Apparently."

"Supper's ready in the dining room."

The dining room felt date-like. Sacha rarely used it, usually eating in the kitchen or at his breakfast nook. Or on the patio or in the living room. In his bed. Hell, anywhere other than the dining room. He led the way.

"Thanks again for allowing me to hang out," Corrigan said, situating himself at the table. "I'm pretty sure all this seems weird to you."

Sacha smiled. "Not especially. I've had a few clients to go on the lam before."

"It must be interesting being a lawyer—lots of compelling cases."

"It can be."

"Was there ever a time that you considered doing anything else?"

Sacha paused with his fork suspended midair as he pondered the question. He thought hard. He remembered his classmates from grammar school on career day stating they wanted to be astronauts and firemen, but not him. Attorney had always not only topped his list but been his entire list. There had been no plan B.

And that brought him to a question both his brother and cousin had stirred in him. Was he an attorney because he wanted it for himself or because his parents had mapped it out for him? Had he simply followed the path like a good little foot soldier? But if he wasn't an attorney, what would he be?

"I suppose not," he finally answered.

"Must be nice knowing your dream and not having to depend on chance."

"What do you mean?"

"Hockey's a coin toss. As a lawyer, you could go

anywhere and set up a practice. You could even do it virtually if you wanted. You don't need agents or get stressed out about being picked for a team. Age and injury aren't issues."

"Law is more competitive than you think."

"I'm not implying that it isn't, but there are so many more options. There are over two hundred law schools in the US"—according to the poster in the law center lobby that boasted ULSA as being ranked the ninth top law school in the nation—"so unless a person is a complete idiot, I'm sure they'd manage to get into one. And there's no limit to how many lawyers there are. Compare that to thirty-two NHL teams with a roster limit of twenty-three. Of course, there's also the AHL and ECHL that add roughly another sixty teams, but that's still not half of law schools." He dug into his salad. "And attorneys don't wake up one morning and find that they've been traded to another team."

Sacha nodded. "Valid points. You make a good argument. Maybe you should consider law. You'd make a damn convincing prosecutor."

"Nah, I get stage fright."

"No way."

"Public speaking has always been a dread. I get tongue-tied every time. I have it all perfectly planned in my head, and then out of my mouth comes utter gibberish."

"Didn't you say you were taking an interview course?" Sacha asked.

"Don't remind me. It's horrible. I either freeze up or repeat myself a gazillion times."

"Well, I'm sure you'll get better with time."

Corrigan shook his head. "Time isn't something I have on my side. Nguyen, he's one of my teammates, says only players who ace everything are going to make the starting line."

"Sounds like maybe your coach is looking for character."

"If that's what you want to call it."

"Well, what would you call it?"

Corrigan shrugged. "I don't know. Me complaining?" He took several more bites of food before speaking again. "So, is your girlfriend going to be ticked that my coming over wrecked your plans for tonight?"

Sacha looked up from sipping his tea. "What girlfriend?"

"The beauty you were with tonight?"

A pit formed in Sacha's stomach. "You think she's beautiful?" What was he saying? Of course Mitzi was beautiful. "She's married." *What in the wide world?*

That was not an appropriate response for a rational person. However, it was quite fitting for a jealous one.

Damn, he would go for Mitzi. What hot-blooded male wouldn't?

Wide-eyed, Corrigan stuttered, "O-Okay."

"No, that's not what I meant." He waved his hand. "I mean, she is married, if you're interested."

"Why would I be interested in your girl... lover...?"

"Gads, no! Mitzi's my sister."

"Oh, well, that's good to know."

"It is?"

"I mean...." Corrigan's cheeks reddened. "It's good that you're not involved."

Sacha's eyebrows lifted.

"I mean, with someone who's married... not to you."

"Oh. I see." Sacha stared down at his plate, not knowing how he felt about this exchange. A part of him was relieved that Corrigan wasn't interested in Mitzi—at least, he didn't think he was. Then there had been a glimmer of hope that Corrigan could be interested in him... maybe. But then he'd added the whole "not to you." What the whole hell did that dangling participle or whatever part of speech it was mean? Was Corrigan saying he was relieved that Sacha wasn't having an affair with a married woman? Or did he mean he wasn't attracted to Sacha?

Shit! He was more confused now than he had been seconds ago. One of the first rules in defense law was not to ask questions he didn't already know the answer to, but fuck this.

"So, to be clear, you're not interested in Mitzi."

Corrigan raised his hands in surrender. "Simmer down, overprotective brother. I'm not going to try to hit on your sister. Yeah, she's pretty, but she's not my type."

"What is your type?"

Yep, that fell out of his mouth. His mouth was officially disconnected from his brain. He'd likely regret asking in a minute judging by the stare Corrigan was giving him. Granted, the question was forward and a bit rude. Okay, a lot rude.

I've lost my ever-loving mind. He had no clue what he was doing. Was it creepy to have offered Corrigan a safe haven for the night and then to hit on him? If Kian's lifestyle was that of a typical—if there was any such thing as *typical*—gay man, boldness wasn't a recessive trait. But he wasn't Kian, and Corrigan wouldn't be a hookup.

Well….

Shit!

Corrigan

HAD HE HEARD CORRECTLY? SACHA WANTED TO KNOW his type? And why? Was he emitting some type of vibes? And what about the vibes he was sensing from Sacha? Call him crazy, but he detected something a little more than the overprotectiveness of a sister. It was almost as if….

If he gauged the situation wrong, this would make for a completely thorny and uncomfortable weekend or worse. Sacha could ask him to leave. But Corrigan was taking huge leaps when he needed to take baby steps. Was Sacha someone he could trust to disclose his sexuality?

Corrigan straightened in his chair and studied him. Yes, he believed Sacha was trustworthy. Lawyers knew how to be discreet. They took oaths of confidentiality.

Next question. Was he a homophobe? He didn't appear to be, but that didn't make him gay. Nothing about Sacha screamed queer, except maybe his fashion sense. But that, too, was an antiquated stereotype. Plenty of straight men dressed well and had high-décor homes. Of course, they probably weren't discussing throw pillows and placemats regularly, but that didn't translate to a thrift store sofa with a hodgepodge of accessories in a room. Besides, Sacha likely had a professional interior decorator design his home. Undoubtedly, he entertained wealthy friends and clients. He wouldn't live like a hobo.

Finally, and the biggest question, if he came clean, what were his prospects of landing a catch like Sacha? As much as Corrigan would like to believe himself not to have an ego, he did. Rejection would be a hard pill for him to swallow.

"I'm sorry," Sacha said.

Corrigan realized a considerable—more than socially acceptable—amount of time had elapsed since he'd been asked the question. He'd sat stunned with a dumbfounded expression. He took a deep breath and exhaled slowly. He couldn't fathom he was about to say what he was about to say.

"Men," he finally replied. "I like men." Another lapse of silence passed before Corrigan asked, "What about you? What's your type?"

"I'm still figuring it out," Sacha admitted, "but I'm willing to explore."

"Curious, huh?"

"No, it's more than that." He folded his hands in his lap and interlocked his fingers. "I've had feelings for years that I've never owned up to or acted on. The attraction to men exists."

"But?"

"Some people have fantasies, but they never live them."

"Why?"

"Fear, most likely."

"Of what?"

"Judgment."

Corrigan smiled sweetly. "That's kind of ironic, isn't it? A lawyer afraid of being judged?"

"It is. But it's also if I try it and don't like it, then what? Where does that leave me? The fantasy would be blown."

"So you'd rather not know?"

"No, I'm not saying that. It just makes proceeding a little more complicated for me."

"What makes you think you wouldn't like it?"

"Well, I haven't liked it much with women." Sacha covered his mouth, as though he hadn't meant to say that aloud.

That was some confession, and Corrigan was unsure how to respond. "I'm sorry?"

Lowering his hand, Sacha refocused on his food. "It's not your issue."

"No, but maybe I could help."

17

SACHA

Help? What did that entail? Here it was—the moment he thought he'd been waiting for, and the *yellow-belliness* sprouted in him. He had no one to blame but himself. He'd opened this can of worms by asking the question. He'd bared a part of himself that was intimate and personal. It had all sounded easier in his head. But once the words were out, it was something entirely different. Now he was unsure how to proceed. In a courtroom, he always felt in control, familiar, and safe. At present, however, he felt vulnerable and exposed in uncharted territory. Normally, if he felt his cross wasn't going as planned, he'd ask for a brief recess to regroup.

Ducking his head and swallowing, he attempted

to suppress his unruly emotions. "I need to check on dessert." He pushed away from the table and stood on unsteady legs. *One foot in front of the other*, he ordered himself, making his way to the kitchen without bursting into a sprint. *You like him, and he seems to like you. Stop being a candy-ass.* Opening the oven, he checked on the peach cobbler inside—his easy go-to dessert when he needed a sugar fix in a hurry. The timer indicated thirty seconds remaining, and he determined that was close enough, as the cobble's crust was nice and golden. All it needed was time to cool—sort of like him. Grabbing a pair of oven mitts, he removed the dessert and set it on the stovetop.

Pivoting to return the mitts to the drawer, he came face-to-face with Corrigan and froze. He was close. Tremendously close. So close that Sacha could see the subtle shift in darkness around Corrigan's irises and feel the soft puff of his breath. And that look as Corrigan's stare dipped to Sacha's mouth… he recognized that stare. It was one of someone about to kiss him.

Oh God. Am I ready?

A lump formed and lodged in his throat.

"Um… it, uh, needs to cool," Sacha stammered.

"Oh," Corrigan replied with a nod, an expression

of uncertainty crossing his features. "Cool." His voice wavered. Taking a step back, he leaned against the island. "It looks… delicious."

"Mm." Rolling his lips in, Sacha stuffed the potholders inside a drawer. *Chicken liver!*

WHAT WAS HIS PROBLEM? WHY DIDN'T HE TRUST himself? Corrigan had been right there… willing. And how had he responded? Made some idiotic comment about a peach cobbler.

Sacha flipped from his stomach to his back and stared at the ceiling as he replayed the kitchen scene in his head on loop, dissecting every second and regretting not having the courage to allow events to unfold naturally. What could have been a romantic dinner had transformed into a PTO luncheon—polite, dull, and gauche.

As he adjusted the pillow beneath his head, an alarming thought occurred to him. Perhaps in the past, he'd been aware of his sexuality and run from it. But was sexuality something a person could outrun?

His fault. All his fault. He'd created this situation, and the most frustrating part was he didn't know why he'd done it. All he'd had to do was allow Corrigan's plush lips to meet his.

Closing his eyes, he allowed himself to sink deeper into that thought, which quickly transformed into a wanton fantasy of Corrigan's lips all over him. How would he feel? Taste? Groaning, he screwed his eyes tighter, as if the act would block the heated images in his mind in the same manner it did the moonlight streaming through the window. Before he realized it, his lips parted to the air, and wistful moans floated from his throat. His palm resting on his stomach drifted slowly toward his groin. He presumed Corrigan would have a firm grip and agile fingers and that his hands would be rough, raking over his skin. As the images in his mind grew more vivid, the twitching between his thighs intensified.

"Oh, Corrigan," he sighed, clasping his semi. Since it had been a while since he'd pleasured himself, he reckoned rubbing out a quick one might help. Maybe that was his problem—he'd gone too long and had become too wound up to process information clearly. According to some experts, sex improved memory. At the very least, relieving himself would facilitate sleep. A hearty orgasm always knocked him out for a couple hours.

"You called?"

Sacha's eyes flew open as his head simultaneously snapped toward the voice coming from the doorway —his wide-open door that he'd not thought to shut. *Fuck!* Living alone, he didn't have a need to close doors for privacy. He snatched his hand from his crotch and sat erect in the bed—though that wasn't the only thing erect. Heat threatened to set his face aflame.

"Don't stop on account of me." Corrigan approached the bed. "I didn't mean to interrupt."

"Did you need something?" Sacha managed, his voice quite shaky.

"I found this." Corrigan held up an object.

Sacha squinted, attempting to make out the form. "What is it?"

"Sorry, I forgot you wear contacts," Corrigan answered, stepping closer. "It's your watch. It was in the bed."

"It must have fallen off when I was changing sheets."

"Must have." Corrigan now stood beside the bed and stared down at Sacha. "I'll leave it here." He placed the smartwatch on the nightstand.

"Thank you."

Silence ensued for a beat.

"It's late. I should get some sleep," Corrigan said

after several moments.

"Okay," Sacha answered, almost inaudible. "Don't let the boo hag ride you."

Gazes locked, neither moved, and another silence filled the space. Sacha could hear his own heartbeat in his ears. He didn't know what to do next. Or did he? Assuming he didn't, he knew the two of them couldn't remain as they were.

Corrigan broke the silence.

"May I ask a question?"

Sacha nodded, uncertain if he could muster an even tone. Did he want to answer questions? "S-Sure."

"Were you thinking about me just then… when you were touching yourself?"

"What would you say if I were?"

"I'd ask if I could watch."

Oh, hell!

Instead of verbally responding, Sacha relaxed his head against the pillow and pushed a few fingers under the waistband of his sleep pants. Even with Corrigan so close, without his glasses and nothing but the dull glow of moonlight as the sole light source, it was difficult for Sacha to see Corrigan's reaction. However, he could palpably feel Corrigan's eyes gawking at his hard-on.

"Lower," Corrigan urged at Sacha's hesitation to continue. He sat beside him on the mattress.

Curling his fingers around his shaft firmly, Sacha slowly stroked upward and hissed as his hand returned to the base. He smeared a trickle of precum across his crest and down his length, relishing the friction of flesh on pulsating flesh. In a matter of seconds, he'd grown to his full length. The idea of being watched had Sacha turned on, but Corrigan directing what to do kicked it up another notch. In all his previous sexual exploits, Sacha had been in charge. To his surprise, he didn't find playing a less dominant role objectionable. However, this was likely due to it being Corrigan. Had it been any other person, Sacha wouldn't have been as trusting. While being with Corrigan did make Sacha nervous, it simultaneously made him comfortable.

A strange type of fear ebbed in him. Venturing into the unknown offered no comfort, but the exploration of something new roused enthusiasm. In his head, things were safe. What he was engaging in now was undeniably not safe. Yes, Sacha was a ball of contradictions tonight that he couldn't explain.

"Does it feel good?"

"Mm." Where were his words? Why could he no longer put together a coherent sentence? His mind sifted through more than a dozen protests he should have been making. Instead, he continued to gaze into Corrigan's ebony eyes as he massaged his cock.

"Let me see. Pull yourself out."

Sacha obeyed and pushed his pajamas and underwear beneath his balls. Something about being partially clothed made him feel more exposed than being completely naked.

Corrigan rested one hand beside Sacha's thigh while the other hand found the hem of Sacha's T-shirt and grazed the velvety skin beneath, coercing another moan from Sacha.

"Do you have any lube?"

"In the nightstand drawer beside you."

The drawer was as neatly arranged as his electronic cords had been. Corrigan discovered not one but three tubes of lubricant. He read the labels and paused before grinning uncontrollably. "These are all flavored." Opening the one labeled mint chocolate chip, he sniffed it. "Do they taste the way they smell?"

"They're pretty accurate."

"Pistachio," he read aloud. "Better hope no one has an allergy to *nuts*."

"If they did, they wouldn't be in my stash."

"Here, then." Corrigan squirted a glob of gel in

Sacha's hand. "Rub it around good. Make it nice and wet."

The dirty talk was something new for Sacha too. Rarely was he vocal in bed, but when he was, he'd been careful not to offend the genteel nature of his female partners. None of them had been into that sort of thing—not that he'd tried often. But he was finding it to be a turn-on, and he obeyed the command, slathering the lube from the swollen, almost purple head of his cock to his sac.

"Good," Corrigan continued. "Now stroke faster."

Sacha's eyes began to close as he increased his pace.

"No," Corrigan ordered. "Look at me. I want to see you when you come."

Mewling softly, he reopened his eyes with a mixed expression of concentration and desire and focused on Corrigan's face.

Corrigan returned his hand to the exposed part of Sacha's abdomen and tenderly traced the light line of auburn hair that ran from his belly button to his patch, charring a path of electric sensations as he went. He leaned in close to Sacha's ear, blowing on his lobe, and whispered, "Faster."

Sacha thrust harder into his fist, and his breathing reduced to panting. "*Kee-yaw.*"

"Look how tight your balls are. It won't be long now, will it?"

Well, it probably would have been had Corrigan not said anything, but his husky voice combined with his combing fingers and warm breath tossed Sacha off the cliff of no return. Grunting, Sacha was overtaken by a throbbing release that hurled him into spasms of ecstatic pleasure and delight. Semen pulsated from his slit in long streams in quick succession. He struggled to keep his eyes open.

And just when Sacha thought he'd finished, Corrigan said, "That was fire." Then, to Sacha's amazement, Corrigan raised his hand to his mouth and licked off the semen that had landed on his hand, sparking another spurt from Sacha's dick.

"Oh, *mon Dieu!*" Sacha exclaimed, blinking.

"So, do you think you're ready now to explore what it's like being with a man?"

He nodded as he regained his breath. "I think so."

"Good. Let's start here." Leaning forward, Corrigan sucked Sacha's bottom lip between his teeth and gently nipped it before licking the seam of his mouth.

Sacha responded by opening on a gasp, and Corrigan slipped his tongue inside. Their tongues tangled together in a wild and raw dance, and the faint scruff on Corrigan's cheek abraded Sacha's jaw. The kiss wasn't how Sacha had expected; although, he wasn't exactly sure what it was he *had* expected. But he had no complaints and was disappointed when Corrigan pulled back and stood.

"Good night, Sacha."

"What you said? Why are you leaving?"

"Baby steps."

Baby steps my foot! Sacha had gotten a taste and wanted more. Now.

Hopping out of bed, he stood in front of Corrigan, his clothing still disheveled. "Look, I don't know how this works, but I'm pretty sure it's rude and not proper etiquette for me to show you mine and you not show me yours."

Corrigan laughed. "You want to see?"

"Oh, I more than want to see. *Je voudrais* to taste."

18

CORRIGAN

"ARE YOU SURE ABOUT THAT?" CORRIGAN ASKED, licking his lips and closing the space between them. He wanted more as well, but he also didn't want to push Sacha too far too fast. Unlike a popular gay stereotype, Corrigan had no problems with taking things slow. While he had no qualms with promiscuity, random hookups, and quickies, not all gay men were about that life. It was also a lifestyle that didn't coordinate with his plans. Multiple partners were fine... until they ran their mouths.

"Positively," Sacha answered, his voice saturated with lust.

Corrigan placed his hand on Sacha's shoulder and gently pressed down. Understanding, Sacha dropped to his knees and looked up through his lashes, to which Corrigan almost lost all control.

What a visual.

Rushing his hands up Corrigan's muscular thighs, Sacha dragged Corrigan's shorts and boxers down his legs to his ankles. Corrigan's cock sprang up and rested on the flat of his abdomen.

"Holy hell," Sacha muttered, smacking his lips.

"It's all yours. Don't be shy now."

The briefest moment of hesitation flicked in Sacha's eyes before he swiped his tongue across the slit to lick away the salty precum, circled beneath the rim, and then closed his mouth over the crown with a slurp. Normally, Sacha maneuvered with polished, graceful movements and seamless effort, but now, Corrigan watched as he clumsily fumbled with inexperience. Sacha appeared to have no inkling of what he was doing, but the gleam in his eyes indicated that he was determined to compensate in enthusiasm for what he lacked in skill. Corrigan observed intently, his eyes blurring with bliss, as Sacha took as much as he could in his mouth, which was about half, and wrapped his hand around the exposed shaft. Pulling his hand toward the base, the saliva allowing for an easy slide, Sacha squeezed and sucked hard before pulling off the tip only to take him in again.

"Geez!" Corrigan cried, his thighs jackknifing forward reflexively. He plunged deep into Sacha's mouth and hit the back of his throat.

Sacha made a choking sound.

"Sorry."

He wasn't. Although he hadn't meant to hurt him, hearing Sacha make that sound perversely heightened Corrigan's arousal even more. Additionally, Sacha hadn't seemed to mind because he hadn't stopped. On the contrary, he continued bobbing up and down and rolling Corrigan's member around in his mouth like candy. With each tug and pull, Sacha's suction grew tighter, and his pace increased. Obviously his learning curve was short, and it encouraged Corrigan to thrust in earnest.

"That's so good," Corrigan whimpered shamelessly. It had been too long since he'd been touched this way. As a result, his desperate pent-up longing caused him to lose control of his body. His hips jutted and grinded in Sacha's mouth as if on autopilot. Everything within him began to tighten. To maintain balance, he dug the pads of his fingers into Sacha's shoulders. "That's it."

He attempted to roll and pull out of Sacha's

mouth but was too late. A deep, thunderous wave of a glorious orgasm rumbled through him, and he watched as his seed seeped from the corners of Sacha's mouth. And although he'd just come, the sight had him stiffening again.

Sacha rocked back on his heels. Red splotches stained his cheeks as evidence of the effort he'd put forward. "That was... was...," he stammered, his voice hoarse.

Corrigan nodded, his senses calming as the rapturous pulsations of his climax subsided. "Yeah, it was."

———

CORRIGAN HADN'T EXPECTED SACHA TO BE A cuddler. Yet here he was with his body slightly curled, his head pressed against Corrigan's chest— his long lashes brushing against his skin—and an arm draped across Corrigan's midsection as they lay in Sacha's bed. Due to Sacha's stillness, Corrigan assumed he'd fallen asleep, but when Corrigan shifted to slide out, Sacha's arm tightened around his waist.

"Where are you going?"

"To get water, but it can wait." He peered down at Sacha's silhouette. "How are you feeling?"

Sacha glanced up at him. "What do you mean?"

"It was your first gay experience. Are you okay?"

"You don't have to treat me with kid gloves. Geez!" He rolled onto his back. "It's not like you deflowered me or anything. Besides, I'm ten years older than you."

Corrigan's brows bunched. "What does age have to do with anything?"

"I'm the elder. I should be teaching you, not the other way around."

Chuckling, Corrigan caressed Sacha's biceps. "I don't know if that statement's ageist, but it's something not right." He allowed his hand to trail up Sacha's shoulder to the rear of his neck and tangle in his hair. "I'm only asking because at dinner you seemed unsure."

"That was dinner, not what we did." A defensive tone had entered his voice.

"I don't mean to offend you. I just don't want you to have regrets."

"Do you? Regret it?"

"Of course not. Actually...." He shifted and kneaded Sacha's pectorals with his free hand. "I was hoping for an encore."

Sacha's eyes widened. "You mean I didn't suck at it?"

"Oh, you definitely *sucked*. You were like a freaking car vac." He hummed with a broad smile. "And your tongue... so wicked."

"But I gagged. I didn't take all of you."

"I don't think anyone is able to deepthroat on the first go. It takes practice. But if it makes you feel any better, I'm willing to let you practice on me anytime."

Sacha grinned. "How generous of you."

"Yeah, I'm a nice guy."

"You are." Tilting his head back, he raised his chin toward Corrigan.

Responding, Corrigan leaned forward and pressed a lingering kiss on Sacha's lips. It wasn't something he typically did with his lovers—not that he'd had many in the past or that he could call Sacha a lover. Well, maybe. Calling him a hookup felt wrong. Sure, they hadn't known each other long, but it already felt like more than a hookup. Corrigan felt a connection. But he couldn't ignore that Sacha was new at this. Undoubtedly, he'd want to explore... experiment... with other people. Besides, how was Corrigan supposed to balance dating—gay dating at that—with being on a conservative—overly conservative—hockey team? If, that was, Sacha even wanted to date. He hadn't said anything about wanting to date. In fact, Sacha hadn't said anything about anything. For all Corrigan knew, Sacha might have decided this was a one-and-done, that he'd satisfied his curiosity and moved on. Maybe being with men wasn't something Sacha wanted to continue.

Corrigan allowed the kiss to end. *Fuck. Things just got complicated.*

Not wanting to pressure Sacha but also not willing to continue playing out scenarios in his head that could probably win an Academy Award, Corrigan decided to pry. "So, did you get anything figured out? Cure any curiosity?" he asked.

"As a label, I'm pretty sure I'm queer."

"Pretty sure?"

"Well, yeah. It's hard to explain. I've never not liked women. I've just not enjoyed them sexually. But could I fall in love with a woman?" He shrugged. "Hypothetically, I suppose so. That would mean maybe I'm asexual or aromantic. But I've never been content in a relationship with a woman. It's why they've always ended. I've grown accustomed to being alone, but I wouldn't call it being content. So, that blows that theory. But what we did…." Sacha smiled. "I really liked it. Does it mean I'm gay?" He shrugged. "I swear I'm too old to be trying to figure this stuff out."

Corrigan chuckled. "You're never too old."

"When did you know?"

"Maybe always, but junior high for sure. One weekend, some friends and I went to an anime expo. We got separated, and as I wandered around looking for them, I stumbled across a comic book booth. What drew my attention were the number of colorful flags draped around the display table." He shook his head. "At the time, I had no idea they were pride flags and thought they represented foreign countries. I mean, I'd only ever seen the one rainbow flag. I didn't know there are over fifty flags that represent all the different groups in the LGBT+ community. I even asked one of the workers if the comics were in English. I guess he figured out what was going on in my head, because he laughed and assured me that they were. Anyway, he asked me what type I liked—shojo, kodomomuke, and so on."

"That's English?"

Corrigan chuckled again and combed his fingers through Sacha's hair. "It's Japanese and refers to the drawing style. Anyway, after chatting with him for a while, I purchased a few that sounded interesting. Halfway through the first comic, it dawned on me that the two main characters, both men, had an interest in being more than friends. And then I realized how much I was rooting for them to get together. When I flipped the last page and saw the two of them lip-locked, I literally fist-pumped the air. It was odd because all my so-called friends constantly made homophobic jokes and talked about how gross it was for two men to be together. And I never said anything about it."

"You were young."

"Odd how people always find reasons to excuse deplorable behavior. It was wrong, no getting around it. Yet my friends somehow made me feel that what they were saying was natural. Reading how that comic book relationship unfolded did something for me, though. Until then, I'd always had a feeling deep down that I didn't belong, that I was different from my friends. They were starting to get into girls, and I wasn't. I tried faking it for a while, but it all blew up when one of my friends had his first boy-girl party, and they decided to play a kissing game. I had to kiss one of the most popular girls in school. It was awful—not because I was inexperienced but because nothing about her appearance or personality appealed to me." He shivered at the memory. "Later that night, I signed into a comic book's fan video chat group. I'd become a part of that online community. And that's when it hit me, I mean really hit me, how close I'd gotten to some of the members. There was this one guy who I thought about all the time. And like the comic book characters, I wanted to be more than friends with him."

"Were you?"

"We sexted some, but that was the extent of it. He lived in San Diego. With the time differences and both of us having our own stuff going on, it was never going to work."

"Hm." His body tensed slightly.

"What?"

"Sexting. Do you do that often?"

"No. Do you?"

"Never."

Corrigan's eyes widened. "As in ever?"

"As in, why would I want to?"

"It can be fun."

Sacha merely grunted in retort.

While the response shouldn't have bothered Corrigan, it had. Perhaps Sacha did have a low libido after all. Corrigan wasn't sure how he felt about that. Could he be involved with someone who didn't desire sex? All his relationships involved sex. Sometimes they were exclusively restricted to sex.

Cripes, I sound like a sex fiend.

"I'm going to get that water now," he said, slipping out of bed. "Do you want one?"

"No, thanks."

He took his time making his way to the kitchen. He needed time alone to think and consider what came next. Were these red flags Sacha was throwing, or was this a matter of him crawling into his head and misreading the situation? He'd come to ULSA to play hockey, not to get wrapped up in an unsustainable relationship with a sugar daddy.

Yikes! Did I just refer to Sacha as a sugar daddy? No, that was not what he meant. Though someone with Sacha's means would be able to toss money at any given situation or feel they could purchase anything or anyone. But Corrigan wasn't there for handouts. He hadn't fooled around with Sacha as some strange obligation of gratitude for allowing him to stay the night. Had he? No, of course not. Corrigan shook the thought from his head.

Reaching the kitchen, he removed a bottle of water from the refrigerator and sat in the dark at the counter. *Stop this,* he warned himself. His thoughts ping-ponged from one extreme to the next. On one hand, Sacha remained uncertain about his sexuality, meaning he may not want to be involved with Corrigan. On the other hand, what if Sacha did want to take this thing between them further? How would Corrigan keep it a secret from his teammates with his coach apparently having spies all over the fucking place?

It's one night. It means nothing. But it did mean something. Though *what* it meant, he wasn't sure.

After finishing his water, Corrigan returned upstairs. His first thought was to go to the guest bedroom and pretend none of this had happened. If it didn't happen, he didn't have to sort through it. However, he walked to Sacha's room.

On his stomach, Sacha sprawled across the bed, his knee bent and hands stuffed beneath the pillow. The steady rise and fall of his chest indicated he was asleep. For a moment, Corrigan watched him from the doorway before quietly making his way across the room and slipping beneath the top sheet.

19

SACHA

SACHA STARED AT THE SHAPE OF HIS MOUTH IN THE foggy mirror as he brushed his teeth. Giddy was how he'd describe himself. His mouth had kissed another man, wrapped around a cock, and swallowed semen. He'd only hesitated due to performance anxiety, not because he hadn't wanted to. But now, the morning after, standing in his bathroom with nothing but a damp towel slung low around his hips and shaving cream slathered across his face to soften his overnight growth, he wondered about his giddiness. Was it the man who made him feel renewed? Or was it the feeling of having performed an act so unlike himself? Or maybe he was having some sort of pre-midlife crisis. Instead of buying sports cars, he was fooling around with a guy ten years his junior. Well, more than that, but ten was a depressing enough gap without mathematically calculating any further.

What was it about Corrigan Ellery that made Sacha lower his inhibitions? No, he wasn't fooling himself. He knew how prudish he could be—not about others but rather the standard to which he held himself. He wouldn't have done what he did with just anyone. If he was certain of nothing else, it was that.

But was this thing—whatever it was—even viable? Corrigan had plans to go off and play hockey. Why start something with someone who would be leaving eventually? And Sacha had his busy career to consider. Would he have time to see where this would lead?

Well, yes, now that he thought about it, remembering his career was in the toilet.

He spat toothpaste in the sink, rinsed, and returned his toothbrush to its holder. Because he felt like being a rebel, he skipped flossing. Why the hell not? He padded his way to his walk-in and selected clothes for the day. Normally he reserved Saturdays at home as days to lounge around in his most comfortable boxers and bathrobe while writing closing arguments. But having a houseguest, he wanted to make an effort to look decent. He didn't want to scare Corrigan off; although, he feared he may have already.

A weird kind of tension had cropped up between them. Sacha could feel it when Corrigan got out of bed to get water last night and again this morning when he'd returned to the guest bedroom to work on a hockey assignment. Sacha supposed it could be true. He'd no reason to believe Corrigan would lie to him. But who the hell worked on the weekend? Well….

Sacha sighed, wandered back to the bathroom, and retrieved his razor. He did, that's who. He used to be the guy who worked on weekends. That was why he'd gone all out designing his home office—a room he utilized more than any other in his house. At least he used to. But now look at him. He frowned in disgust as he scraped the razor across his stubble. What use was that home office now? Fuck up and this was what happened. That was the price of being a Weymouth. He'd give anything to have his old position back.

But wait. Was he replacing his job with an affair? Was Corrigan a placeholder or a gap fill-in for being ousted from the firm practice? Maybe not completely ousted but close enough in his opinion.

Dammit!

Rinsing the razor, Sacha continued staring at himself. Why was he still so confused? At present he couldn't even get his morning routine together, aimlessly roaming about his closet and bathroom. Being angsty wasn't like him. In courtrooms, he knew all his moves and his opponents' moves before they occurred. Yet in his home, in his personal life, he was baffled by nearly every fucking thing.

Pull it together.

He finished his shave and trudged back into his walk-in. Plopping on a plush ottoman, he pulled his knee close to his chest and studied his neatly clipped nails. He'd been annoyed that the nail salon hadn't had his usual jojoba foot soak and had substituted with rosemary and tarragon. Pretentious? He was pissing himself off.

He could have a far worse life. He'd made the grades and gotten the LSAT score, but truthfully, his father's check and donation had probably held more weight with the admissions council. He hadn't had to compete for a position in the prestigious law firm; his surname had guaranteed him an in. And even his being booted hadn't left him jobless or destitute. Yet here he was whining and feeling sorry for himself— agitated because his father had snatched his job from beneath him and his last night's lover had pulled away. Ticked because he'd taken the first step and not gotten what he wanted. Spoiled. Entitled. How dare his life be messy.

His vision flooded red, and impulse overtook him. Multiple conflicting and opposing emotions warred within him. Retrieving a nearby shoe, he hurled it across the room. It crashed into the wall with a loud thud, bowling over several hats on mannequin heads, and shattered one of the glass doors to his suits' enclosure. The sound shook him back to reality, and he stared at the destruction as if caused by someone else.

Great. Now I have to clean that up.

Seconds later, Corrigan, wide-eyed, appeared in the doorway. "Geez!" His gaze darted from Sacha to the broken glass and back again. "Are you okay? What happened?"

Sacha flushed with embarrassment. "Stupidity and existential neuroticism." He stood and moved toward the debris.

Corrigan grasped Sacha's upper arm and held him still. "You'll cut your feet."

Sacha nodded and blew out a bitter laugh. "I do bleed like everyone else."

"Huh?"

Shrugging, he met Corrigan's concerned eyes.

"Nothing. I got this. You should go back to doing what you were doing." He tilted his head. "What are you working on, anyway?"

Corrigan shuffled and groaned. "Right now, training is mostly about conditioning and technique development and not so much execution of plays. Coach is seeing who works well together, how players play off each other's strengths. So I have to make a list of all my strengths and weaknesses."

"That doesn't sound too tough."

"I also have to do it for every member on the team—at least five things listed in each category. Plus, I have to write a plan of correction for all the weaknesses, i.e., what can be done to improve them. Whatever I write will be implemented during the fall. So, if I say I need to increase my speed and that running five miles daily will help do that, then that's what I'll have to do all semester."

"Still, that doesn't sound bad. You want to be your best, and you're working toward that currently. So what's the problem?"

"It's not just what I list. Everyone's opinion is being taken into consideration. So if the majority thinks I need to go rock climbing every week, rock climbing it is."

"Someone would really suggest rock climbing?"

"I don't know. Maybe."

"I take it you wouldn't be thrilled if it was."

"Do you like it?"

"I've never been, but my brother's brother-in-law loves it. He's climbed K2 and Annapurna. But I get what you're saying. Your teammates could hang you out there if they want, and you'll have no say."

"That and the fact that I'll have to read aloud everything I list about everyone. It'll be as pretty as popping a zit."

"Criticism can be harsh, but if it's constructive, it'll only help you improve. And that's the ultimate goal, right?"

Sacha reflected on his own words. Perhaps his father's point had been valid. Maybe there was more Sacha could have done to prevent what happened with his client from happening. Maybe he deserved the demotion.

"I know. Doesn't make it any easier, though."

"No, it doesn't."

Corrigan's eyes scanned down Sacha's torso to the towel. With his knuckles, he skimmed from Sacha's hip to his navel. "For a lawyer, you have some decent abs."

"Racquetball," he answered, attempting to squash the quake in his voice stemming from the simultaneous shiver and heat skittering across his skin at Corrigan's touch. "I play a couple days a month." He neglected to disclose his doing so was solely to justify paying the outrageous fees for his country club membership his mother insisted he keep. "Maybe you and I could—" Sacha stopped abruptly. No, they couldn't.

Weymouths were generational members, practically a mandatory staple. His children's children's children were already welcomed, but Corrigan wouldn't be. Only now did Sacha realize how little he cared for the place and why. How had he allowed himself to be a part of an organization with such fucked-up restrictions without noticing?

Note to self: cancel membership on Monday.

"On second thought, I don't enjoy racquetball all that much."

"Then why do you play?"

Sacha hunched his shoulders. "Because my brother does."

Corrigan smirked.

"What?" Sacha asked.

"Nothing," Corrigan replied, shaking his head, his grin widening. "Well, maybe. Do you ever say no to your brother and hold to it?"

"Certainly." *Well, not always. Sometimes. Okay, no.* "What makes you think I don't?"

"From the way you talk, like about attending your sister's party or going to your parents' house for your brother."

"That's what family does." He didn't want to discuss his family, and Corrigan appeared to pick up on that.

"Okay." Corrigan inched his knuckles closer to where the towel was tucked in. "There seems to be something protruding beneath your towel."

"Maybe you should examine it. You know… for scientific purposes."

Corrigan chuckled and inhaled deeply, seemingly savoring Sacha's scent of fresh soap and shampoo. Leaning close so his lips were only a hair away from Sacha's ear, he asked, "Science?" He hooked his index finger in the towel.

The warm tickle of Corrigan's breath on Sacha's earlobe combined with the delicious tease of his touch propelled frissons of desire through Sacha's body. He should be getting dressed, cleaning up the mess he'd made. Returning phone calls. Anything but this. Hadn't he just demolished his damn closet door because he was spiraling? But instead of pulling his shit together and using any type of judgment, all he could think and feel was how much he wanted this man.

"Back in my day, all majors required a science course."

"Uh-huh." Corrigan plucked at the soft cotton, and the towel plunged to Sacha's feet. "Oops."

20

CORRIGAN

STARING AT THE TOWEL CRUMPLED ON THE FLOOR, Corrigan released a dithering hiss. Hadn't he convinced himself that he wouldn't do this? That he wouldn't involve himself with someone who was playing sexual orientation bingo? And that he would allow Sacha space to sort through his doubts and feelings? But more importantly, to protect himself from being crushed if Sacha reverted to his heterosexual lifestyle? Sure, perhaps it was a hypocritical stance for Corrigan to take since he wasn't scaling the Empire State Building, waving a rainbow flag, and screaming his favorite color was glitter. Yet he wasn't crouched in a dusty, cobwebbed closet either. He knew how he identified and was comfortable with it. The fact that he lived in a world where he didn't feel free to openly express it was another matter entirely.

On the contrary, Sacha couldn't admit to himself how he felt because he didn't know.

Corrigan knew the pain well of a person who was unsure of himself. He'd watched his father struggle with it daily for years after his accident. Each day, he didn't know the father he would wake up to. Would he be kind and joking, making the most of his situation? Or would he be cranky and insolent, incensed that he could no longer perform the mental or physical tasks he once could? Indeed, part of his father's issue was the result of brain injury, but not all of it. He took his frustration of uncertainty out on those around him, and that wasn't something Corrigan wanted to experience with Sacha.

On the other hand, Corrigan wanted Sacha with every fiber of his being. The very thing that repelled him from wanting to take things further with Sacha was the exact thing that drew him in. He couldn't help feeling drawn to him on both a physical and emotional level. There was something about him that fired up parts of him that no one else did and made him want to ignore all the red flags to run. If Sacha wanted to explore, Corrigan wanted to go along on the expedition and be his tour guide of pleasure. As an overall picture, it didn't make sense. Then again, weren't athletes stereotyped as not smart?

He glanced at the shattered shards of mirror on the floor. "Are you sure you don't want to talk about why you're destroying your closet?"

"It's just a mirror."

"It brings bad luck."

"Hockey players are always superstitious, aren't they?" He shrugged. "I had a moment—a stupid one—but it's gone now that you're here. You don't have to worry. I'm usually not reckless. In fact, everyone says I'm exactly the opposite, that I'm always careful and never do anything out of the ordinary."

"Oh, I have to disagree with that last part... unless having a 'physics lesson' in the buff is what you consider ordinary."

"Well, if it's okay with you, I'd rather pretend it never happened and proceed with other *teachable* moments."

"It's okay with me."

Corrigan dragged his fingers across Sacha's hip to the small of his back and tugged him forward, closing the gap, but not close enough that their bodies met. There was no resistance in Sacha, and a small, tortured sound escaped him that caused Corrigan's full, sultry lips to quirk at one side. No amount of prudence would stop him from diving into this jumbled mess. The animalistic urge to ravage the attorney was too great.

"C'mere," Corrigan growled, crushing his mouth against Sacha's, and melted. His tongue delved into the warmth of Sacha's mouth. Nudging Sacha's knees apart, Corrigan stood between them with his erection pressed firmly against Sacha's thigh. All the emotions he'd been harboring—confusion, hesitation, frustration, and irritation—evaporated in a moment. This felt right. "I need to collect data," he uttered.

If scientific proof was what Corrigan sought, he found it in physics. Newton's third law of motion theorized that for every action, there was an equal and opposite reaction. Corrigan's greedy kisses were matched with Sacha's hungry ones. His moving back and forth against Sacha was equaled with Sacha's hips grinding against the rigid muscles of Corrigan's thigh. Their tongues teased each other with maddeningly dawdling strokes while their hands groped and fondled each other.

"How far do you want to take this?" Corrigan managed.

"As far as you're willing to go."

"Are you sure?" Corrigan's hand rushed up Sacha's torso and cupped his throat with enough pressure to cause Sacha to tremble, startled. Being the stronger and more dominating of the two, Corrigan could overpower Sacha, rendering him helpless in minutes if he squeezed harder. However, Sacha's eyes glinted with excitement and awe, indicating he was ready and willing for anything Corrigan decided to offer. Although Sacha nodded, Corrigan already had his answer.

"Never more positive."

With a slight shove from Corrigan, Sacha landed in a reclined position on his elbows on a chaise lounge. Taking a step forward, Corrigan tugged his shirt over his head and heard Sacha's breath hitch. It gave Corrigan pause only for a second before he toed off his shoes and unbuckled his jeans.

"Gravity," he said, allowing the denim to fall to the floor. "That's more science."

"It certainly is."

Never breaking eye contact, Corrigan reached into his boxers and stroked his hardened shaft. "Would you call this antigravitational pull, then?"

"I'd call it still too many clothes."

"Oh, in that case…." Corrigan pushed down the underwear and stepped out. "Better?"

"Much."

Straddling Sacha, Corrigan gazed at their swollen cockheads and the fat veins that lined their shafts. The sight was almost enough to make him lose it, and his entire body vibrated at the contact. However, he contained himself. Wrapping both his palms around their shafts to form a sheath and using their leaking precum as a lubricant, Corrigan rubbed them together as if they were one. At the same time, he rotated his hips, pressing their balls together and simulating penetration. The growl that tore from Sacha's chest sent Corrigan into a frenzy of thrusting.

"Not this soon," Sacha begged in vain as he pushed against Corrigan's shoulder. "You've got… you have to slow down or…." He gasped for breath between each word. "*Mon Dieu*, you're going to make me come."

"I know. Eventually."

Sacha's expression of panic, lust, and exhilaration thrilled Corrigan but didn't worry him. He'd always possessed a canny ability to sense how much he could tease his lovers before cascading them over the brink. Sacha wasn't there yet; therefore, he pumped them together several more times before abruptly standing.

"What's the matter?" Sacha whispered.

"I have a taste for strawberry."

Grasping Sacha's hand, Corrigan led him from the walk-in to the bedroom. With a salacious grin, he retrieved a packet of strawberry lubricant and a condom from the nightstand. Instead of applying the lube directly to Sacha's groin, he squirted a generous amount above his navel and watched it slowly slide to Sacha's auburn thatch. Sacha moved his hand to massage it in, but Corrigan slapped it away.

"Don't you dare."

"You're teasing," Sacha hissed after releasing a dramatically long breath.

"Guilty as charged, counselor," he replied, squeezing on more lube. "Get used to the slow burn your body will feel." He licked a line along Sacha's jawbone to his ear. "I'm going to do all sorts of naughty things to make your dick twitch," he cooed in Sacha's ear before nipping his lobe. "And you're going to beg for all the pleasure." That if he didn't find himself begging first. Corrigan monitored Sacha's reaction to the statement for any reluctance, again not wanting to push him too far too fast. Sacha's dilated pupils indicated he was into it and spurred Corrigan to continue. "You're about to be schooled."

"Do I need a safe word or something?"

Corrigan's eyebrows arched. "What do you know about safe words?" Not that he thought Sacha was virginal, but he'd always pegged him as a vanilla kind of guy.

"Just that some couples have them."

Couples? Corrigan was too invested in his own lust to analyze Sacha's use of the word, but it wasn't completely lost on him.

"Sure, we can have a safe word. What do you want it to be?"

Sacha shrugged. "Jalapeño?"

"Jalapeño?" Corrigan chuckled. "Why?"

"You know." Shuffling, Sacha hooked his arms around Corrigan's neck. "For when things get too hot."

"But you don't mind spicy, right?"

"Call me cha-cha." He emitted a hissing sound.

Thank fuck. Corrigan questioned if he'd be able to temper his urges to mild.

Pressing his body against Sacha, Corrigan gyrated his hips to spread the lubricant between them while digging his fingers into Sacha's ass enough to leave a mark. "Jalapeño it is."

Sinking to his knees, Corrigan ripped open the foil packet with his teeth and inserted the tip of his finger into the reserve. Being sure not to break eye contact, he placed his finger between his lips and teeth, positioning the condom in place. He then lowered his head over Sacha's penis and in one swift motion used his lips to carefully smooth the latex over the supple mushroom crest and down the shaft.

"Oh my fucking word!" Sacha squeaked, his breath erupting in a thick gush.

"Let's get you ready to go." Corrigan smacked both palms against Sacha's ass and drew him forward. Interlocking his fingers behind his back and taking his hands out of the equation, Corrigan swirled his tongue hungrily over the head, causing Sacha to hum with pleasure. With the momentum of his upper body, he bobbed his head, sucking deeply and controlling the rhythm and depth despite Sacha's hip thrusts. Slow and firm. Back and forth. Corrigan allowed himself to relish each pull and the feel of Sacha's smooth, rigid flesh. When Sacha teetered on the brink of release again, Corrigan pulled off and stood.

"Wh-What?" Sacha questioned with a dizzy gloss in his eyes.

Taking more of the lube, Corrigan smeared it

across his own rear before slicking it over Sacha's fingers. He bent across the footboard, wiggled his ass, and looked over his shoulder at Sacha. "You need to prep me."

For a moment, Sacha looked like a deer in headlights before something seemed to click, and he moved forward. Timidly, he pressed the tip of his forefinger against Corrigan's puckered hole. However, Corrigan reached around, grabbed Sacha by the wrist, and bucked back so that Sacha's finger aggressively plunged in up to the knuckle.

"You won't hurt me," he assured, rocking across Sacha's digit.

The reassurance worked, and Sacha inserted a second finger and then a third, shoving them in and out with quick, hard strokes. A tingle began building inside Corrigan as Sacha's fingers brushed across the outer nerves. It didn't take long for him to be completely relaxed.

"I'm ready," he panted, looking in the dresser mirror for a full view. "Go hard. I like it hard."

Placing his hands on Corrigan's hipbones, Sacha breached Corrigan's hole—the first ring of muscles giving away to the pressure and burn of being stretched. Corrigan's lungs ignited in his chest, and his forehead beaded with a sheen of perspiration. He couldn't describe what he felt. All he knew was he wanted it to continue. He needed it to continue. He needed deeper. He needed faster.

"Move," he demanded, rocking back as far as he could and not waiting to adjust to Sacha's size. "Take my ass. Own it."

Although Corrigan instructed Sacha to up the pace, it was Corrigan who controlled the movements. He pumped hard against him, sliding all the way to the tip and then bucking back to have Sacha's balls slap against his ass.

Yes, yes.

Sacha grunted and swore behind him. At least, Corrigan thought Sacha may have been swearing. The few words that were in English were incomprehensible, not that they needed words in this moment.

"I… I…." Sacha's grip tightened on Corrigan's hips. "Ooh," he drew out.

Corrigan felt Sacha's jerky movements behind him and watched in the mirror Sacha throw his head back with a hoarse cry, an expression of delight and agony on his face. Corrigan allowed Sacha no time to collect himself before he moved off and pivoted around to face him. He shoved him onto the bed and kneeled over him. Wrapping his big fist around his girth, Corrigan pumped himself furiously until he saw a white-hot oblivion of fireworks, and his ejaculation exploded from his prick onto Sacha's chest.

As the haze of euphoria faded, Corrigan stared down at Sacha. "You're going to need another shower."

21

SACHA

MONDAY MORNINGS IN THE LAW CENTER USUALLY blew chunks in every direction except the right one. However, after the weekend Sacha had, his tolerance for the day was better than normal, though he wasn't sure why. He'd eaten good food and slept soundly. He'd streamed several entertaining movies and even had delightful conversations with Corrigan. But they hadn't discussed their... situation. After their Saturday morning romp, they'd avoided the topic altogether. Corrigan had returned to the guest bedroom to work on his class assignment while Sacha had piddle-paddled around the house, cleaning and ordering shit off the internet he didn't need—although, the retro gauge kettle and toaster set he had coming were going to look bomb in his kitchen. Of course, for the ridiculous purchase price, the appliances should also take out his trash, wash his windows, polish his silverware, and mow his lawn.

The "morning after" awkwardness that had developed between him and Corrigan surrounding the topic not discussed was a problem sure enough, but not enough to prevent Sacha from enjoying Corrigan's company. It merely dampened it, and Sacha remained without answers.

And perhaps that was why he hedged away from answering questions—because he knew if Corrigan asked certain ones, he couldn't provide a valid answer. What he did know for sure was he felt something for Corrigan, something deeper than anything he'd ever felt for a woman. In the past, if he'd developed some type of emotional attachment to a woman, he hadn't been too broken up about it if his feelings hadn't been reciprocated. He wouldn't classify any of his splits as emotional but rather inconveniences at times. Other times, they came as a relief. He'd been more bothered by being not bothered—so unbothered that deep down, he'd begun to wonder if he was a sociopath unable to connect with people. But there existed a difference between unable and incapable. He did form meaningful relationships, just not romantic ones.

Besides, what was the point of drudging up his shit when he and Corrigan had completely different trajectory paths? The young buck was trying to get to the pros. He had a college degree to obtain and wild oats to sow. He didn't need some dude barreling toward midlife holding him back or suffocating him.

At what age does midlife start, anyway?

Yet it didn't diminish or negate what Sacha felt—his want and need to be with Corrigan. But obviously, Corrigan was comfortable with random hookups. He'd demonstrated that by the ease with which he'd walked away. Twice.

Sacha exhaled. Maybe it wasn't important to have all the answers and all that was needed was to live in the moment. Only, it felt important to him.

His thoughts were interrupted by his ringing cell. From the tone, he knew it was Kian.

"You're up early," Sacha greeted, acknowledging the two-hour time difference.

"Yeah," he sighed. "I'm still working that crazy missing welfare money story. It's actually why I'm calling."

"Ah, and here I thought it was my sexy telephone voice that allured you."

Kian chuckled. "Phone sex is passé. I'd be more interested in your dexterous texting fingers."

"Oh, you talk so *puurrty*. Speak to me, Daddy."

Kian laughed again. "You're a nut. But speaking of nuts, how are yours?"

"Attached."

"You liberated those suckers recently?"

"We weren't discussing my sac."

"Doesn't mean we can't."

"And it doesn't mean we should."

"Did you know the most frequent cause of death for men under forty is an excessive buildup of cum?"

"Stop making up shit."

"I'm an investigative journalist. I research these things."

Sacha rolled his eyes despite Kian not being able to see him.

"I'm telling you," Kian continued, "not getting laid is unhealthy."

"Well, in that case, I should pass a physical." He heard a thud on his best friend's end followed by a brief silence.

"You're shitting me. You legit got laid? As in, had

sex? With someone else? Besides yourself? And not a doll?"

"You asshole." Sacha attempted to sound annoyed but failed.

"Who was she?" Kian sang. "Anyone I know? Someone from the office? You know, office romances never work out."

"Geez, I miss you."

"You're deflecting."

He was.

"Come on. Who was she?"

"*He* is someone you don't know."

"Oh shit!"

This time Sacha heard a loud crash, as if several objects had fallen.

"Are you for real? A guy?"

"Yes, yes, already. Don't act so surprised. I told you it was a possibility."

"No, you said you had thoughts, and I never thought you would act on them. Wait. Is this the hockey player? How was it? Tell me everything. I need details."

"Those you're not getting."

"But I'm your best friend. I'd tell you."

"And?"

"Sacha Yves Weymouth, don't make me blow my

frequent flyer miles just to come and shake the snot out of you. You know I'm that bitch. Now spill it."

"Oh *mon Dieu*, you're so dramatic. You didn't have to use my entire government name." Sacha cradled his phone between his ear and shoulder as he poured a fresh cup of coffee from the pot he'd made in some fancy-schmancy contraption with a gazillion buttons. No way was he drinking the sludge Paxton had left. *What happened to machines where you just pour in water?* "Yes, it was the hockey player, and we fooled around a little."

"Uh-huh." Kian sounded skeptical. "Define *fooled around*."

"You know. Did stuff."

"Dammit, no I don't know. That's why I'm asking."

"We may have kissed and touched some."

Kian gasped loudly. "You fucked him."

"Kian—"

"You did. Fess up."

Nope. Not going there. "Didn't you call for a reason?"

"I did, but this conversation is long from over."

No shit. When Kian wanted information, he was like a dog with a bone and refused to let go.

"So, I've been working on this piece about

welfare funds that are thought to have been misap-propriated."

"What do you mean, *thought*?"

"It's the strangest thing. There's extra money on the books, but no one knows who put it there or where it came from. It's been allotted and assigned to various welfare programs, but those programs never received the funds. It's like ghost money."

"That is odd."

"It gets weirder. Before the money vanishes, it looks like it was invested."

"Well, if it was on the stock exchange, maybe it was lost."

"That's just it. Each investment shows a profit, but the investment company denies handling any funds. Then the loop starts all over. The question becomes, is it a misappropriation of funds if the money should have never been there or never existed?"

Interesting. Sacha sipped his coffee. "Okay, but what does that have to do with me?"

"In my digging, I found a name, a Maude Cheroncourt."

Son of a bitch!

"Didn't you represent a Cheroncourt not too long ago?" Kian continued.

Boy, did he. Harper Cheroncourt Fallon was the reason Sacha was sitting where he was. "Yeah, her great-grandson. He's doing thirty in a federal pen."

"Didn't the family go broke years ago?"

"That was the story. Maude's daughter married an Austrian aristocrat. Any money she had had come from her husband. But after his death, there were disputes with his family about the will, and Maude was awarded a small settlement, only a fraction of his total worth. What's left of that has been divided among her living relatives."

"Hm." Kian paused as if considering. "So, what am I missing here?"

"I couldn't tell you. Harper was charged with tax evasion and racketeering. He swore the only money he had was dividends from his vineyard in Napa Valley and his work as a documentarian. The DA found evidence of several offshore accounts, but by the time they moved to freeze them, all the money was gone. Couldn't locate a single penny, euro, peso, ruble, bitcoin, or whatever currency it was in. Just empty shell accounts."

"More ghost money. Did they find anything?"

"A whole lot of smut. Turned out Harper's documentaries were adult films with some questionable *adults*." He took another sip of coffee. "He swore everyone was of legal age, and no one has come forward—not that they can identify all the actors—to complain. But he shot his movies in locations with very loose age of consent laws. Plus, he may have dabbled in being the CEO of street pharmaceutical distribution. Of course, I didn't learn any of this until the bastard got convicted."

There was a knock on the office door, though the door was wide open. Sacha snapped his head up to see Mace in the doorway and waved him in.

"Hey, Kian, my cousin is here. Let me call you later."

"Sure, no problem. I need to go over my notes now. Thanks for the info."

"Any time, though I'm not sure it helped any."

"I'm not, either, but that's why it's called investigative journalism. Oh, and don't think I've forgotten about you getting your ass cherry popped."

Sasha's face burned with heat as he flushed every shade of red in the color wheel. "That didn't happen."

"We'll talk about it later."

Before Sacha could respond, Kian disconnected.

"This a bad time?" Mace asked, shoving his hands in his tailored pants pockets.

"Nope. I was hanging out in here until everyone else arrives. What can I do you for?"

"Do you happen to have a key to downstairs?"

"The archives?" Sacha shook his head. "I don't, but it all should be cataloged into the computer database. Let me log in and—"

"Don't bother. I already did, and it looks like records are missing. Besides, I don't know what I'm looking for."

"Huh?"

Mace helped himself to a cup of coffee and sat in a chair across from Sacha. "Have you ever had a case where the more you worked on it, the more it tap-danced on your fucking nerves?"

Nearly spitting out his coffee, Sacha choked down the beverage. "Wow, someone must have royally pissed you off."

"Is it too much to ask for detectives and prosecutors to do their damn jobs? I mean, sure, it's job security for us, but damn." His cool tone and relaxed demeanor were in stark contrast to his words. "And if I call that bitch assistant DA out and say she's got sand in her *cocotte* because I've decimated her in the courtroom every time I've gone against her, she's going to cry sexual harassment to the bar."

Dabbing his lips with a napkin, Sacha peered

through his lashes at his cousin. "That's a lot of pent-up hostility for a Monday morning."

"It's been building for a while. Plus, she interrupted my breakfast—caused my eggs and rice with that good Lord and Barrett sausage to go cold. I honestly wonder how she hasn't combusted into flames like a witch roped to a stake the instant she steps into sunlight."

"What has you so peeved?"

"Something isn't adding up." He leaned forward. "My client attended a party the night his parents were killed. Dozens of witnesses saw him at this party. He's even on the marina security footage boarding the boat." Mace counted each point he made on his fingers. "Yet no one sees him return. All the witnesses are missing. And a drug screen indicates positive results for Rohypnol. Instead of this raising a brow for the DA and police, they have a hard-on to pin the murders on my client. Trust and believe, if some of those detectives attempted to throw themselves on the ground, they'd miss—solid proof that evolution *can* move in reverse."

Scratching his chin, Sacha thought for a moment. "What's in the archives that you think will help?"

"That I don't know, but my client did state that the press had gotten a hold of confidential medical records, which are not only protected by HIPAA but also were sealed by courts due to him being a juvenile at the time. Even my client doesn't have a copy of those records, but he knows this firm handled the legal aspects. He doesn't remember doctors' names or hospitals, and I want names. Because if I find out it's a midlevel hospital employee or some coked-out physician leaking information, I'm going to sue them until their dick shrivels up like the underside nut sac of a naked mole rat."

Sacha snickered and crossed his legs. "Now, that's vivid… and specific."

"You know, I'm going to do us a solid and talk to Max about you helping me out on this. I could use you riding shotgun."

Vehemently, Sacha shook his head. "No, don't cause any trouble for yourself. You know what they say about no good deed going unpunished."

"Sach."

"I appreciate it, but it wasn't only my father. It was all the partners. Besides, I don't need anyone's permission to root around in the basement."

"Just a key."

"Correct." Sacha nodded. "People should begin rolling in the next couple hours."

Mace checked his watch and finished his coffee.

"Unfortunately, I can't wait around until then. I have a deposition in forty-five, and then I'm meeting Mother for brunch at some snooty place that's bound to serve scallops that taste like they've been shot from a wild boar's butt." He stood and rebuttoned his coat. "I swear, the elements of the universe have conspired to prevent me from having a decent meal experience today. I'll come back later."

"As I said, I don't mind."

"Okay, thanks. I doubt this is something that's going to be resolved quickly anyway. Something in the milk isn't white, and the math isn't mathing."

"It never is."

22

CORRIGAN

CORRIGAN'S DORM ROOM DOOR SWUNG OPEN without warning, striking the wall with a loud bang. Startled, Corrigan snapped his head toward Nguyen, who now graced the threshold with an ominous expression and a wadded ball of paper in his hand.

"Dude, what did you do?" Nguyen demanded.

"What are you talking about?"

"This." He tossed the paper he was holding on Corrigan's desk. "You gave an interview to Leo Warnock?"

Corrigan smoothed the wad to reveal it was the sports page of the latest issue of the *Minotaur Advocate*. He swallowed hard and gulped a deep, calming breath as he read the headline: **Ellery Top Runner for Captain**.

Shit, shit, shit! Like he needed to add another reason for his teammates to want to gouge out his eyes with a serrated spoon and impale his severed head on a spike.

"What were you thinking?" Nguyen began pacing as Corrigan quickly scanned the article. Throwing his hands up in the air, Corrigan's teammate continued, shaking his head. "This is so disrespectful to all the guys who have been on the team for years. We all work our asses off, but this?" Pointing at the paper, he threw his hands in the air again. "It chucks the rest of us away like rotting corpses in some serial killer's crawlspace."

Corrigan looked up from the newspaper. "I never said any of this stuff. I swear."

"Why would you even interview with him?"

"I didn't. I didn't even know he was a reporter. I only spoke with him for a few minutes at a frat party."

Nguyen's brows bunched. "He was trolling Gamma house?"

"No, the other one. I was—"

"Wait, you went to XDU, the most exclusive and sought-after fraternity on campus?" He squared his shoulders. "Ah, now it makes sense."

"What does?"

"Why you would have an invite. You did this to impress them?"

"No." Corrigan jumped to his feet. "We didn't talk about hockey. I mean, he asked who Coach favored—"

"And you said you."

"No, I told him no one, and that's the truth. Why would you think I'd do something like this?"

"Because everyone knows how much you hate Theriot."

"I don't *hate* him."

"Then why wouldn't you tell Warnock that Theriot's captain?"

"I don't know. I wasn't thinking, I guess." Shrugging, Corrigan stuffed his hands in his sweatpants pockets and swayed. "But is he really? I mean, do we know for sure he's going to remain captain? Or is it like Coach said and no one is secure?"

Nguyen frowned. "Look, I don't know how you did it back in New York, but this for sure isn't how it's done here. Not kosher. We have one another's back."

Seriously? The team has my back?

"For the last time, Bo, I didn't throw anyone

under the Zamboni." He snatched the newspaper from the desk and waved it in the air. "All of this is a fabrication. I mean…." Cursing, he raked his hand through his hair. The accusation in Nguyen's tone should have pissed him off, but Corrigan had to admit that the evidence looked incriminating. Plus, Nguyen really didn't know him—none of his teammates did. There'd not been golden bonding moments. "Factually, everything is accurate—my stats, where I'm from, and all those things. But I never once said anything about me becoming captain."

Nguyen's expression softened. "Coach is going to be furious when he reads this."

Don't I know it?

STANDING IN THE LOCKER ROOM DOORWAY WITH nearly two dozen sets of eyes glaring at him, Corrigan reevaluated his life. His plan was, and always had been, to join a premier college hockey team. Perform impressive work while there. Win a Frozen Four—hopefully two. Get signed by a professional team and go straight into the league as a starter. Gross enough money to be able to make a copious donation to the university like all affluent alumni and perhaps be honored with a building being named after him, or at least a wing. Of course, knowing his luck, he'd only get a bathroom, and maybe not even that—just a toilet: The Ellery Stall.

So when or where in this smashing plan of his had he inserted making friends? Because that shit had derailed before the train had left the station.

"Listen, guys—"

"You punk bitch," Theriot interrupted.

"Cool it, Theriot," Coach Massey ordered, a stern expression etched into the fine lines of his face. "That's no way to speak to royalty."

Oh damn. This is going to be bad.

"For twenty-three years, longer than most of you have been squirted out, I've been coaching, and it never fails that each year there is at least one prima donna who thinks he's All-American and knows how to direct a team better than I do. One who believes he's entitled to any position and doesn't have to *earn* his shift." The coach paced the center of the room, his stare downward at his shoes and hands clasped behind his back. "One who shakes his fist at God as being inferior. One player who is so omnipotent that he possesses the ability to glide on water and resurrect the dead. How blessed the rest of us menial and basement dwellers are to be graced with such eminence. Well…." He stopped pacing and looked up at his players. "I guess that means I have to prove that I'm the man for the job and earn my paycheck. Everyone on the ice in two minutes." He marched out of the room.

"Fuckwad!" Theriot mumbled, snatching his practice sweater from his stall.

"CORNER TO THE HALF WALL TWO VERSUS ONE," Coach Massey barked once everyone was on the ice. He wasted no time pitting Theriot and Kavanaugh against Corrigan.

On the first pass, Kavanaugh left Theriot uncovered, preventing Corrigan from gaining the puck without contact. Theriot, whose job in the drill was to pass to Corrigan, was slow to do so. And when Theriot did decide to pass, Corrigan had to overextend, leaving him off-balance and susceptible to being knocked off his feet—which happened—to reach the pass, only to get clobbered by Kavanaugh again. Any way it went, Corrigan found himself on his backside. And because of his poor performance, Corrigan had to perform the drill again with the next group and the next group and the next, all having the same results.

He got it. Basically, this was Coach Massey's way of allowing the entire team to have free hits on him. Bullying? Probably. But, at the same time, it was hockey—a contact sport. Hockey players had to be tough. They had to be willing to sacrifice their bodies to make plays. Most importantly, Corrigan had to endure if he expected to remain on the team.

Eyes on the prize, he reminded himself as he climbed to his feet from the ice. *Let them get it out of their system. Do not show weakness. Do not break.*

Eventually, the hockey gods intervened, and Coach Massey received a phone call he had to take, allowing the team to take a ten-minute rest break. Huffing, Corrigan made his way to an isolated end of the bench and chugged a sports drink. The cool liquid flowed over his parched tongue so quickly he didn't taste it as it slid down his throat.

"Do you need to borrow my pads?" Larousse asked, removing his helmet and leaning against the wall.

Corrigan responded with a tiny smile. "Wouldn't hurt."

"Well, if it's any consolation, you took that shit like a trooper."

"Thanks." Corrigan watched as two teammates skated past, eyeing him with all the compassion of a viper ready to strike. "Aren't you afraid someone will say something about you consorting with the enemy?"

A wicked expression crossed Larousse's face. "I wish a mofo would. Listen, I know Leo Warnock, and he has a knack for making a story where there isn't one. I suppose that's what he has to do to get anyone interested in reading that rag, but my guess is he wasn't trying to cause trouble. He argued a case for you, and it crawled between some people's butt cheeks."

"But not yours." Corrigan swiped his forearm against his forehead. "Why are you unbothered?"

"I'm a goalie. I can't be captain."

"Ah." Corrigan nodded with understanding. "But if you weren't?"

"Then we might be having a different conversation. Welcome to D1 hockey. It ain't all cotton candy and tata bouey. Fuck what you heard." Slapping Corrigan on the shoulder, he flashed a reassuring grin as he walked toward his other teammates.

"Hang in there. That which does not kill you lets you live to die a gruesome death another day."

"I don't think that's how that saying goes."

"Maybe not, but it doesn't make it any less true."

Survival. That was what Larousse had meant. Corrigan only had to survive.

But what if he wanted to *live*?

23

CORRIGAN

"Get your shoulders over your knees, Ellery," Coach Massey bellowed. "Knees over toes. This is basic edge work. What are you doing?"

If Corrigan had been asked that question two hours ago, he may have been able to answer. At present, his mind was mush and fogged with fatigue. He hiked his back leg higher and skated a backward C-cut on his outside edge left leg before turning and doing the same on his right. The neon orange cones strategically positioned on the ice distorted into clown faces mocking him, and the rink stretched endlessly in front of him like a deserted highway in a B-movie horror flick.

Of course it's endless. It's a circle. Circles are endless.

Well, no. Yes, circles are endless, but hockey rinks are rectangles—so not endless.

He sailed around another cone, leaning in more and feeling his blade bite into the ice. Fifty cones in fifty seconds, the coach had demanded. What was Corrigan on now? Twenty-five? Thirty? What was his time?

Go! he commanded himself. *Just go.* It didn't matter that everything was a blur and that sweat burned his eyes. He turned out his knee and toe and shifted his weight, slicing the ice. Left foot. Right foot. Left. Again and again. Cone after mocking cone.

Did they still think after two solid weeks of riding him hard he'd quit? They were delusional—or maybe he was. After all, he was the one seeing talking heads on this verglas polygon with an infinite number of sides. The sounds of voices, sticks striking against the floor, and metal on ice wavered in and out. His chest rose and fell with heavy but controlled breaths as he glided into the next maneuver, the sting digging into his thighs and glutes. His eyes focused on the obstacle course, making visible the invisible lines he needed to skate. He could do this. He *would* do this. He was living his vision and not his circumstances. Then a whistle blew. *Was that a whistle?*

He stopped, and holy shit, the pain! If he thought skating the drills was agonizing, it was nothing compared to the pain in his muscles when he stopped. He felt as if his lower half had been dipped in molten lava and sprinkled with cactus spines. *Mother of pearl.* He grimaced, clenching his jaws as he skated—wobbled—to the bench to join his teammates.

Suck it up. Don't let them see you hurting. Hold it in. He compressed his lips into a tight line. *Happy thoughts. Think of something happy.* Sacha's face immediately popped into his mind, and Corrigan's heart leaped to his throat.

"Per usual," Theriot sneered, "Corrigan's the last in."

Ordinarily, the statement would have bothered him, but at present, he was too winded and in pain for the insult to fully register. *Blah, blah, blah* was all he heard. Lips moved, but nothing made much sense, and finally, the coach dismissed them. The walk from the ice down the chute became a blur too.

Slouching on the bench in front of his locker, Corrigan fished his cell from his gym bag and smiled at the icon of having new text messages—well, at one in particular. The others—notification of uploads from his favorite YouTubers; messages from Hoyt Lemelle and Alton, two of the guys he'd met at the fraternity party; Panhellenic links for mandatory antihazing and sexual harassment videos—he couldn't care one way or the other. However, seeing Sacha's name, even without knowing the content, made his day.

Although they'd been texting daily since he'd left Sacha's home, he felt a distance—one of his own doing—creeping into their developing... relationship? Was that what they were calling it?

It wasn't fair to pressure Sacha to label himself, and, *technically*, Corrigan hadn't. But he'd walked away and left things as if their time together had been a weekend hookup. With a label, he would feel more... what? Valued? Secure? Assured? Guilt gobbled at his insides for feeling the way he did—to feel so emotionally drawn to Sacha, yet afraid to go all in. Becoming involved with someone sexually ambivalent—if that was the correct word—was tricky. Experiments went left all the time, and he had no interest in becoming a sacrificial guinea pig. Corrigan knew himself all too well. He didn't just fall for someone when he fell. No, he plunged without a safety net. And he felt himself falling harder, faster, and deeper for Sacha than he had for anyone in the past.

He leaned back against his cubby, disgusted. How hypocritical was he? Here he wanted Sacha to figure it all out, but what would Corrigan do if he did? Push him and their relationship into a closet so no one knew? Hide Sacha from his teammates and coaches? Lie about how much he meant to him? At least Sacha was being honest about having doubts about his sexuality. Corrigan knew but refused to admit it to anyone.

Then again, why should he be the only one to throw himself in a pit of fire? What would Sacha lose? He had the security of a prominent last name and generational wealth that could practically buy him anything he desired, including his pick of boy toys. His sexuality didn't jeopardize his future the way Corrigan's did his.

He scanned the locker room at his teammates in various stages of undress. The old, familiar questions cropped up in him again. Would they be uncomfortable knowing a gay man sat among them? Would they fear he was checking them out and awaiting an opportunity to pounce on them in the shower? Were they the kind of people who bought into the deleterious lavender panic stereotype that gay men lacked the restraint to curtail their sexual urges and held a main goal in life of *corrupting* straight men to the "dark side?"

He wouldn't create an opportunity to find out.

"What's up with you?" Theriot asked, planting his hands on his hips. "You about to hurl or something?"

"What's it to you?"

"Because as captain, it's my duty to know players on this team are healthy."

"Well, I'm fine, so you can move on."

Nguyen, undressing beside Corrigan, glanced at the phone in Corrigan's hand and smirked. "Looks like girl trouble to me."

Kavanaugh snorted from across the room. "Ellery with a girl? I doubt he's ever eaten pussy."

Nguyen shook his head but laughed. "Geez, Kav, you have zero tact. You must have been born in a barn."

Tossing his socks in his gym bag, Kavanaugh flashed a devious grin. "Hey, if it's good enough for the Divine, it works for me."

Larousse draped a towel around his neck. "Oh, I know you didn't just make that comparison. Can we leave religion out of this?"

"Yeah," Nguyen agreed, untying his pants. "We have enough issues. Is anyone else wondering how much longer Coach is going to keep trying to invent new ways to kill us?"

"Until," Theriot said, narrowing his eyes at Corrigan, "we look like contenders. Like we belong."

"If you have something to say, say it," Corrigan challenged.

"When I do, I will, but just know, affirmative action isn't going to earn you a spot on my line."

Corrigan leapt to his feet, jaws clenched and muscles coiled, and came eye to eye with the captain.

"Ah." Theriot scoffed smugly. "There it is. There's that bestiality. What are you going to do, Ellery? Hit me?"

Corrigan had a good mind to do just that; however, he reined in his temper after considering the ramifications of his actions and the conditions of his scholarship. He was already at the top of Coach Massey's shitlist. Adding to it would be unwise. But on the other hand, slugging Theriot would be so satisfying that Corrigan could practically taste it.

"I've taken dumps that have smelled better than you," Corrigan clapped back, glaring and not breaking eye contact. "You're not worth the toilet paper to wipe my ass."

Theriot parted his lips to speak but didn't. For a second, his eyes flickered with what Corrigan would have labeled in anyone else as hurt before he spun and walked away to the showers.

Nguyen tapped Corrigan on the shoulder. "Hey, a new zydeco band is playing at Lafourche tonight. A group of us is going to skip the dining hall and go. Care to pass a good time?"

Corrigan's face scrunched in confusion. "What?"

Nguyen chuckled. "Do you want to go, silly?"

"Oh. Um. Maybe. Sure. What's zydeco?"

Larousse gasped. "Saint Cecilia, pray for us, and Ellery especially!"

"You told me to leave religion out of it, and now look at you," Kavanaugh griped as he headed toward the showers.

"What can I say?" Larousse responded. "The boy needs prayers if he doesn't know what zydeco is."

Nguyen followed Larousse. "Cut him some slack. He's from New York."

"Yeah, and it's supposed to be a melting pot *and* populated with plenty of people of Haitian descent," Kavanaugh rebutted. "I'm not giving him a pass. I'm canceling his ass."

Nguyen glanced over his shoulder at Corrigan, hunched his shoulders, and smiled. "I tried."

24

SACHA

Frowning, Sacha waved off his approaching brother. "No," he grumbled, climbing the final two stairs and carrying a stack of journals as part of his glorified stock boy duties. "I've already had my mouth assaulted by a baking soda sandblaster this morning, and I don't need any more fuckshit." He marched down the corridor to the resource room.

Paxton followed. "I haven't said anything."

"But you will, and I won't like it."

"You don't know that."

"The hell I don't."

"Is that any way to talk to the person who got you in to see your first NC-17 movie and allowed you to have the last slice of Patti LaBelle's sweet potato pie at Thanksgiving?"

Sasha drew a face and dumped the books on a nearby table. "Yeah, after you dropped it on the floor."

"Don't be nitpicky. It's the gesture that counts."

Oh, do I have a gesture for you.

"If this is how you're going to behave, I recommend you never go to the dentist again and just allow all your teeth to rot out. You could rock a set of dentures."

Suppressing his urge to smile, Sacha crossed his arms. "Do you even think before you speak?"

"Well, there's always veneers, but you run the risk of making your teeth too big. I mean, you have lips the size of a guppy but a mouth the size of an anteater."

"Why are you still talking to me?"

"Because I need you to watch the kids this weekend."

"You have a nanny."

"And she has plans."

"I might have plans."

"Do you?"

Sacha shuffled uncomfortably. "No, but I could," he muttered.

"Oh?" Paxton's eyes gleamed with intrigue. "Are you seeing someone?"

Shit! He hadn't meant for the conversation to go here. "No. Yes. Maybe." *Fuck!*

"Well, I'm glad that's clear. Does this other person hold the same opinion?"

Hunching his shoulders, Sacha propped himself on the table. "Honestly, I don't know where his head is."

"So it's a *he.* How's that going?"

"I like him… a lot."

"But?"

Sacha shrugged and fiddled with a pencil left on the table. "He's young. Real young."

Paxton's brows bunched in concern. "How young? As in ten to twenty and a lifetime on a registry young?"

"Listen, I may be a touch flummoxed, but I'm not stupid. Or sick. He's legal… well, for some things."

Paxton's brows bunched more. "What?"

"He's twenty."

"Oh." He sighed with relief. "Twenty works… unless he doesn't. He trying to mooch off you?"

"No, nothing like that."

"Then what's the problem?"

"I remember when chatrooms were a thing in the nineties. This guy doesn't know a world where dial-up exists."

"So you're a geriatric millennial. It's not the end of the world. You'll just have to educate him on a few things, which could be fun." Paxton waggled his eyebrows.

"More like he's teaching me."

"Learning can be fun too. But I'm sensing something deeper is bothering you."

"We're at different stages in our lives. He's not going to want to get serious or settle down."

"Whoa. Wait a minute." Paxton held up his hand. "Did he tell you that, or are you assuming?"

"He's twenty."

"In other words, you're being an asshole. You should know better than to stereotype anyone."

Sacha winced at being called out on his bullshit.

"It's called communication, something necessary in every relationship no matter what age the participants are," Paxton continued. "Seems to me, you're creating your own fuckshit."

"Ugh! Stop reading me."

"If this is something you want, which it seems to be, then you're going to have to shimmy into your big boy drawers and work it out."

"You're right."

Paxton's beaming smile returned. "I know. I always am."

Sacha rolled his eyes dramatically.

"Now, will you babysit?"

"Fine. What time?"

"Seven." His smile widened. "So, how's the sex?"

"I didn't say we had sex."

"Yeah, but you did. I can tell because you've been too damn chipper these last couple weeks. I figured it's either because the Hounds have a chance of going to the Superbowl this year—and we both know that ain't happening—or you got laid."

"Sometimes, I really, really don't like you."

Sitting beside him on the table, Paxton patted his younger brother's knee. "This is a big step you're taking, and I want you to know you have my support. But I also want to know you're okay."

"I am."

"The last time we talked about something like this, you admitted that you'd never had a good experience. Has that changed?"

"Yeah. It's good. Granted, it's only happened twice, and there are things I haven't done."

"But?"

"No buts. I can see myself with him."

"Wow." Paxton smiled reassuringly. "You sincerely are smitten."

"It's more than that, Pax. I've fallen for him.

Hard." He shook at the words tumbling from his mouth. It was the first time admitting aloud what he'd been feeling for weeks. "But is it too much too fast? Is it just enthusiasm for a new lifestyle?"

"I can't answer that, but I can tell you that when I met Gretchen, I knew immediately."

"Seriously?"

"Yeah. I let her dangle out there a spell wondering, because you can't lay all your cards on the table the first night. But yeah, she had me from the giddy-up. I proposed on our third official date. Four months later, we were married, and look at us—still here. It doesn't always take the *Iliad* and the *Odyssey* and a Battle of Troy to figure out who you're meant to be with. And you don't need reasons to validate what you feel. It doesn't matter what anyone else thinks. It's what you feel that matters most. There are always going to be people who don't get it, who question the authenticity. People who complain that it happened all of a sudden. But guess what? It's not their relationship, and it's not their place to judge."

"But they will judge. I'm in a position of power… sort of. He's a Croneau Foundation scholarship recipient. At best, it's a conflict of interest."

"Why? Because if you're eliminating dating anyone who has any slim association with this firm in any way, you're back to dating your hand. Our health insurance is good, but do you want to meet your deductible on carpal tunnel surgery?"

Sacha's bottom lip jutted out. "Again, have I mentioned how I don't like you?"

"What else you got that's holding you back?"

Sacha parted his lips to relinquish. "Noth—"

"So, this is your payback to me," Maxwell Weymouth barked, standing in the doorway.

Both Sacha and Paxton hopped off the table as if snapping to attention.

"Father!" Sacha nearly swallowed his tongue. A pit formed in his stomach.

"Paxton, I'm going to need a word alone with your brother."

Distressed, Paxton stared at his brother, his eyes silently communicating that he would only leave at Sacha's request.

"It's okay," Sacha said, nodding slightly.

For a moment longer, Paxton remained motionless before begrudgingly exiting. Once his eldest son had departed, Maxwell one-handedly shoved the door shut.

"I knew," Maxwell stated slowly, his voice low, "that you were upset about the partners' decision to move you. I knew you held me responsible. But never did I imagine you would go to this length to hurt me or this firm."

"What I do in my personal life has nothing to do with—"

"You can't be so ignorant not to know that *everything* you do is a reflection of me and this firm. What do you think our friends will say once they learn of your deviant behavior? Think they'll continue to eat their crumpets and *mille-feuilles* and not be disgusted by the thought of you? Of course, they'll blame your mother and me for raising you around the wrong sort, for allowing you to befriend that Kian boy."

"Kian is one of the most moral and upstanding people I know."

"He's not our kind," Maxwell snapped. "Now he's put these debauched notions in your head."

"He didn't—"

"Shut up!" Maxwell warned, wagging his finger. "I just finished a call with Mace, who expressed his concern that the partners have been too harsh on you and I should bring the matter up for reconsideration. But after learning of your sickening behavior as of late, I'm not inclined to do any such thing until you stop engaging in this filth. Do you think your cousin would have put his good name on the line vouching for you if he knew what you are? It seems you're better here out of sight of everyone. Otherwise, you'll continue to disgrace this family."

"Is that what I am to you? A disgrace?"

"This is not how you were raised. Not only have you demonstrated unabridged incompetence, but you're now exhibiting flagrant doltishness. And if you ever want to be reinstated in this firm, you *will* end your foolish, vindictive licentiousness immediately."

Sacha attempted to keep his voice even, not from anger—which he was—but from the sadness that was stomping his soul. "It's illegal to hold my sexuality against me."

"Your sexuality?" Maxwell snorted. "You were transferred due to your failure and blatant inadequacy to perform. There's no mention of your *sexuality* in any records. None of the partners know— that is, unless you've told them. And I doubt informing them will improve your situation."

"You'd do this to me? Your son?"

"No son of mine would behave the way you have."

Don't cry. Don't cry. Sacha fought back tears swelling in his eyes.

Pivoting, Maxwell opened the door and left.

Shortly thereafter, Paxton reentered and rushed to his brother's side.

"Are you okay?"

Unable to speak, Sacha nodded.

"No you're not," Paxton replied, his voice laced with bitterness. He pulled his brother into a tight embrace.

25

CORRIGAN

AFTER SOME THOUGHT, CORRIGAN HAD A CHANGE OF heart and decided against going out with the team. Sure, it would have been an opportunity to bond, but why bother? Day in and day out, he spent his time with these people, and nothing changed. Besides, his body ached. The hot shower had done little to soothe his aching muscles, and he had a ton of reading to do for classes. And if he were going to spend the night out, he'd prefer to do it with Sacha, but that wasn't going to happen. For now, he was resolved to sit on the bench in the empty locker room, embrace the silence, collect his thoughts, and rest his muscles before making the long walk back to the dorm. However, a slamming door interrupted his plan. He looked up the same moment as Theriot rounded the corner lockers.

Well, hell in a handbasket.

Theriot startled. "What are you doing here?"

"Minding my own business and leaving yours alone."

Theriot grunted and then mumbled under his breath, "No need to be nasty."

"That's funny coming from you—a person who rarely has a civil word for me. Of course, why would you when you hardly think *my kind* is human? We're just a bunch of jungle monkeys, right?"

The color drained from Theriot's face. "You don't know me or what I think."

"Don't I? I think you've made your opinion clear from day one."

"No you don't. If you did, you'd know…." Shaking his head as if he'd had another thought, he shrugged. "Forget it," he mumbled, taking a step away.

Corrigan moved in front of Theriot, blocking his path, and crossed his arms. "I got time."

"I'm not that way, okay?"

Something in Theriot's tone made Corrigan want to believe him. Or maybe he wanted to believe him no matter what—that he wanted to find the good in everyone and not believe that in this age, people still treated other people as less than human. Perhaps he wanted the optimism of Anne Frank. However, this was Theriot, who'd never given him reason to believe anything different than the ugliness he'd displayed.

"Well, you're doing a damn good impersonation of it. Maybe you should test your skills in Hollywood."

"Maybe." He moved to step around Corrigan, but Corrigan moved with him, continuing to block his path.

"What, you're not so bold without an audience?"

Theriot sighed. "Just drop it." Again, he moved, and Corrigan blocked the way. "Look, it was never my idea."

Huh? Idea? "What wasn't?"

Closing his eyes, Theriot released a long breath before meeting Corrigan's gaze again. "None of it. I'm not supposed to tell you, but before you arrived, Coach called me into his office and told me to go in on you to toughen you up."

What the hell? Corrigan's mouth fell open. Would his coach seriously advocate something so depraved? Only one word came to mind. "Why?"

"Coach said we needed to do it before the other teams did, that they would say those kinds of things to goad you into drawing a game misconduct, and it would destroy you and this team. He said it would be your Achilles' heel and an easy target."

"And you willingly went along with it?"

Theriot shook his head vehemently. "No. I wanted no part of it, but Coach said it had to be me because as captain, the other guys would follow my lead." He dropped his gaze. "You don't know how sick it made me to spew such filth. He convinced me that it was for the best and that there was no other way."

Corrigan plopped down on the bench, his eyes glossed with disbelief and astonishment.

"I'm truly sorry if I've hurt you." Theriot sat beside him. "I just...." He stared at the ceiling as if searching for an answer. "It's hard saying no to Coach. I know that's no excuse, and I should have refused. But sitting in his office, listening to his rationale, it all made sense at the time. Tough love. Trial by fire. My father taught me to swim by tossing me in the Caney."

Silence emerged while Corrigan allowed Theriot's words to sink in. A swirl of emotions numbed him. Everything he thought he knew had been turned upside down once again. His coach had orchestrated the hell he'd been living. Was this a moment when the end justified the means if it was for a better good?

From his peripheral vision, he regarded Theriot, who looked as if he'd had his soul eradicated, and Corrigan's mood sank further. Why did he feel pity for the captain when moments ago he'd wanted to strangle him?

"You seriously didn't mean any of it?"

"Not a single word... well, except for you being slow. That part is true, but none of the other stuff. In all fairness, though, you have improved and are keeping up better now."

Corrigan nodded. He had improved, and for what it was worth, Theriot's taunting had become less distressing.

"So, can we start again?" Theriot's tone didn't exude the confidence of receiving a positive response. "I mean, we are stuck on the same team until I graduate."

"That's if Coach doesn't cut me."

"He won't. You're one of the best players we have."

Corrigan huffed, but his eyes widened at the unexpected compliment. "Tell that to Coach. I'm on the fourth line."

Theriot smiled knowingly. "No you're not."

"Yes I am. Where have you been living? I'm—"

"Do you genuinely think Coach would delegate Hansford and Kavanaugh to the fourth line?"

Hearing Theriot ask aloud drove in the ridiculousness of the notion, and Corrigan shrugged.

"Coach said it would make your line work harder if you thought you were fourth. He's grooming y'all to be a rotating first with my line. He thinks it'll give us more options."

"He sure keeps you in his confidence, doesn't he?"

"Only because he does a lot of his bidding through his captains. But it's like being a puppet sometimes."

Another silence ensued for several minutes before Theriot stood. "Look, I know it's a lot to ask, and I don't blame you if you say no, but I'd like for us to try to be, if not friends, at least cordial."

Corrigan nodded. "I can do that." And he could.

"C'mon. I'll give you a ride back," Theriot offered.

"Thanks." Corrigan gathered his belongings.

26

SACHA

"So you're just going to give up? End things?" Paxton asked.

"I don't see that I have much choice," Sacha replied, staring into the garden koi pond and swirling his bourbon in the glass. His mood had called for a drink stronger than beer. "Father has made his position exceedingly clear."

"And that's it? You sacrifice your happiness to indulge Father?" Paxton shook his head. "You can fight this, you know. Fight him. Legally—"

"It's not that."

"Then what is it? You said you care about this man."

"I do."

"Then what? You'd rather have a career than take

a chance with someone who's possibly your soul mate?"

"He *is* my soul mate." His own words stunned him, and he froze. When had he decided this? And even so, what possessed him to speak it aloud?

"Then why, Sacha? Why do this?" Paxton pressed.

"Corrigan is a Croneau Foundation scholarship recipient. Father could make life very difficult for him... find a way to strip him of his scholarship."

"Why would he do that?" Mace asked, entering the garden and removing his designer sunshades.

Sacha and Paxton grew quiet and turned at the unexpected arrival of their cousin, expressions of startle and discomfort on their faces.

"Sorry," Mace said, picking up on the tension. "Gretchen told me y'all were out here. Am I interrupting? Because I can leave."

"No, you're fine," Paxton replied, waving his cousin toward them. "I could use backup to reason with this knucklehead. How much did you overhear?"

"Only that Max will possibly interfere with the distribution of foundation funds." The fading sunlight glinted off his gray hair as he tilted his head. "My question is why."

Paxton turned toward his younger brother. "Do you want to tell him?"

Panic streaked through Sacha. He loved and respected his cousin the same as he did his siblings, and he held Mace's opinion in high regard. He appreciated Paxton leaving him the decision whether or not he wanted to come out to Mace. And Sacha did want to do that. He didn't like having secrets from his cousin, yet saying the words terrified him. He couldn't take any more rejection.

Mace picked up on the hesitation, and his eyes softened. "You don't have to tell me. Listen, I should go."

"No." Sacha grasped Mace's wrist as he turned to leave. "I want you here."

Nodding, Mace sat at the garden table and crossed his legs. "What's happening?"

"Father has disowned me."

"What in heaven's name for?" Only people who knew Mace well would have detected his outrage in what outwardly appeared as an unphased demeanor.

"I'm...." Sacha cleared his throat and collected his nerves. "I'm dating Corrigan Ellery."

Mace nodded slowly. "I see. And this Corrigan Ellery is a scholarship recipient?"

Sacha nodded.

"Well, I assume since the scholarship is awarded to college students that he's at least eighteen."

Sacha nodded again. "He is."

"Well, that makes you both legal adults. Scholarship recipients are decided by a board—which you're not a part of—based on the merit of application and recommendation. Did you know him before he was awarded the scholarship?"

"No."

"I see no impropriety. So, what's the problem?"

"He's a *he*," Sacha said.

Mace shrugged and waited for further explanation.

"I'm queer."

"Okay, I get that, but what does that have to do with the foundation?"

"Homophobia," Paxton interjected. "Father's threatening to block Sacha from ever returning to defense law in the practice if he continues dating Corrigan."

Mace's eyebrows pulled together. "That's preposterous. Besides, there's no such thing as homophobia. Phobia suggests fear. This is plain ignorance."

"I agree," Paxton said. "But Sacha here is going to end his relationship."

Mace focused on Sacha and completed Paxton's

thought. "Because you think if you don't, Max will eventually go after your boyfriend."

"I don't think it, Mace. I know that's what he'll do."

Mace shook his head. "He won't."

Sacha's eyes lifted. "What makes you so sure?"

"Because I represent Timothée Croneau, who is now the current president and CEO of the foundation. And for reasons that I can't explain due to lawyer-client confidentiality, I can say with the utmost confidence that my client would not be pleased to learn that he's overseeing a foundation with biased practices. While his mother may have held alliances with this firm, Timothée Croneau does not. He would have no problems taking his business elsewhere should such information *just so happen* to find its way into his inbox." Mace's lips curled upward slightly. "So, rest assured, he's no one Maxwell wants to offend." He leaned forward and patted Sacha's hand. "Don't let your father stand in your way—not on this."

"But he could still make trouble for him. I don't think Corrigan is out to his team, and you know how jocks can be."

"True." Mace nodded. "But again, I don't think

Max will want to go there. He'd be *honte* and would rather amputate a testicle than air family laundry."

"Unfortunately," Paxton said on a sigh, "we can't force the partners to let you back in."

Sacha set his glass on a table. "As long as Corrigan's safe, the rest doesn't matter. He's what's important."

Corrigan

As Theriot crossed the parking lot to Beauvais Hall, he looked to his right at Corrigan. "I'm glad we're getting a chance to start over. Honestly, I think it'll be better for the team if we're not at each other's throats constantly."

"I agree, but will Coach? He won't be happy that you're not following his orders."

"Maybe." Theriot hoisted his duffel bag higher on his shoulder. "But he's also always talking about oneness and the importance of being a team. As captain, it's my job to ensure we all come together."

"*As captain.* You say that a lot."

"A lot comes with it. It's not just a letter stitched

on a jersey or a chick magnet. Maybe one day it'll be your role."

Corrigan rubbed his hand on the back of his neck and winced. "About that newspaper article... I truly didn't—"

"I know."

"You do?"

Theriot nodded. "Anyone who takes that much shit at practice and doesn't beg for forgiveness is either a masochist or telling the truth. Besides, Larousse hit me up. He explained about Leo. Do you think you're the first player to get misquoted?"

"I wasn't quoted at all."

"It doesn't matter now. It's over. Time to move forward. Coach got his pound of flesh."

"And then some," Corrigan grunted.

Theriot chuckled. "You're a tough cookie, Ellery. Most would have broken weeks ago."

Cocking his head, Corrigan stared evenly at his teammate. "Is that the goal? To break people? Because I thought you said it was to toughen me up."

"It's both. Look, Ellery, this hockey program is bigger than both of us, bigger than Coach. Millions of dollars ride on us, and the powers that be are determined to squeeze out every miserable cent. That means casualties—good players pushed until they have nothing left to give. It means a billboard of shiny stars. They'll pamper us when we win and punish us when we don't."

"By billboard, you mean Coach's favorites?"

"I don't know if *favorite* is the appropriate word, but the ones who become the face of the team, yes. Players who motivate the boosters to dig deep in their pockets and the university to avoid cuts."

That resonated with Corrigan. "Yeah, makes sense. Sacha said as much."

"Sacha? Is that your boyfriend?"

Corrigan stopped in his tracks, his eyes wide as saucers. "What?"

"The guy with the Mercedes."

Corrigan's mouth hung open.

"Come now. Did you think I wouldn't know?"

"I never…. But how…?"

"How many times must I tell you? I'm captain. It's my job to know everything going on with this team. I'm my brothers' keeper."

"But you hadn't said anything, never used it against me."

"I also told you I'm not a complete dick. It's not my place. How you crumple your sheets is your business."

"Does Coach know?"

"Probably, but who knows? But listen, if any of the guys on the team ever try to give you shit about it, let me know. I'll take care of it."

Take care of it? Who is this guy?

Speechless, Corrigan nodded and willed his feet to start moving again. Stunned by the revelation, it hadn't crossed his mind to refute the allegation. Frankly, it was a relief that someone knew.

Only... was Sacha his boyfriend?

"The guys can talk all the shit they want to about me, but Sacha's off-limits. If anyone comes for him, I'll slam their ass to the asphalt like a skateboard."

"I doubt that'll happen," Theriot continued. "It's not like you're the only person on this team who has a boyfriend."

Wh-What? "Who?"

Theriot tilted his head and grinned. "I'm not telling."

27

SACHA

SACHA HELD HIS HAND BENEATH THE FRIED GREEN tomato to catch any dripping remoulade and stared across the room at the taped box on the table. It wasn't much. He hadn't brought much when he'd transferred to the law center because he hadn't thought the move was permanent. The fact that he hadn't been assigned an office gave him hope of a short stay, and he'd temporarily stashed his belongings on a corner table in his father's office. When he'd moved in, he'd thought he hadn't brought enough. Now he was thankful he hadn't. It simplified moving out.

He would have been gone hours ago if Paxton hadn't bought him lunch as a bribe to stay until the end of the day. How was it possible that his entire life could be accumulated in one measly box? Sure, there would have been more boxes if he'd packed up his house, but how much of any of it would have significance to his impact on the world?

But *did* he impact the world? Did his life have meaning? Purpose? Or was he just a paper punch—one teeny circle cut from a flat, blank sheet with so many others? Insubstantial and unremarkable? Would his legacy be notable, or would he be forgotten the second his warm corpse hit the ground?

Contemplating life curtailed the enjoyment of his lunch, and he shook away the thought. He'd made a vow to step away with dignity and the type of elegant discretion his cousin frequently displayed. Few people recognized when Mace was flustered, and his impassive expression pissed them off. Not that Sacha was aiming to tick off his father—although that would definitely be a bonus—he simply didn't want to appear beaten by someone who obviously held him with little regard. Had his father ever loved him? He had to wonder, because it didn't seem feasible to him that anyone who truly cared for him could withdraw affection so easily.

Suddenly, an epiphany flittered in his mind, and Sacha stopped chewing. Perhaps he had suppressed acknowledging his sexuality because deep down he knew his father's convictions and had wanted to circumvent his rejection. And not only his father. His mother would be aboard too. She had supported every action Maxwell Weymouth had ever taken. He'd seen her quickly recant opinions—and not out of fear—once she realized her husband held an opposing stance. Perhaps Sacha had transposed this deep-seated fear of rejection onto his budding relationship with Corrigan. Maybe he snubbed the thought that Corrigan could care for him because his own father didn't.

Well, fuck! I have daddy issues. How fucking cliché?

A knock on the door snapped him from his thoughts, and he looked away from the box to his father's paralegal standing in the threshold.

"I'm sorry to interrupt your meal. Your father gave me a list of errands. I was about to go do them, but someone is here asking to see you. He doesn't have an appointment. What would you like for me to tell him?"

Sacha didn't feel like seeing anyone, but he also didn't want to inconvenience a student. Since classes had begun, he'd found that many students preferred to meet with him than his father—although, he couldn't argue that he blamed them. Many were confused by the syllabus and already overwhelmed by the readings. He could empathize, reflecting on his days of first-year law.

"You can send him in."

"Would you like for me to stay and answer the phones?"

"No, I can handle things. And you don't have to rush back. Take your time."

She smiled sweetly at him. Sacha knew his father didn't treat her well or pay her nearly enough for what he had her do. He returned her smile.

"Thank you."

"It's nothing." Grabbing a napkin, he wiped his hands and mouth, then closed his boxed meal.

"Hey," Corrigan greeted, stepping into the room and closing the door behind him.

Sacha's smile widened, and a warmth filled him. "Well, hello. I wasn't expecting to see you."

"I have a break between classes and thought I'd stop by. I was going to use asking for a fraternity letter of recommendation as an excuse. I've decided to pledge—not that I have much choice. They don't seem all that bad after all and may actually be fun. But the truth is I wanted to see you... since you're not responding to my texts."

Guilty. Sacha hung his head. Since his blowup

with his father, he'd been avoiding Corrigan. "Yeah, I'm sorry about that. Things have been a little crazy these last few days."

Corrigan tilted his head. "Are you sure that's all it is?"

"What do you mean?"

"Things got a little weird between us."

"Weird?" Sacha raised his brow.

"Tense. I guess I freaked out a little." He shifted his weight. "I had a plan to come here and play hockey. I never thought I'd meet someone like you and develop such strong feelings."

"You have feelings? For me?"

Corrigan shifted again and shoved his hands into his pockets. "Here's where I start to sound like a cheesy greeting card commercial. The thing is, I never believed a gay man would be accepted in hockey. I was struggling with that and resigned to keeping my personal life on the down-low. Then an amazing man who I thought was far out of my league enters my life and adds a completely new set of concerns. What if I take the risk to come out, and you aren't in it for the long haul? What if you're just... curious? Where does that leave me if you decide this isn't the lifestyle for you?"

"Cor—"

Corrigan raised his palm. "Wait. Let me finish. I realize now how selfish that was, and that's not what love is about."

Sacha blinked twice. "Love?" he croaked.

"I totally get it if you don't believe me. I know it's fast, and you may think I'm too young. But *I* know what I feel. And I want to move forward with you no matter the consequences. Any doubts or problems we encounter, we can work through them... together."

A moment of silence ensued.

"Say something," Corrigan urged, his voice cracking.

"Well...." Sacha moved toward Corrigan. "I like this commercial, but I'd prefer it to be a feature film. I don't know the right thing to say other than I love you too. Plain and simple. I want to be with you. Build a future with you. Be the creepy old man with the hot boyfriend."

"Stop insisting you're old. I got my first off-the-books paying job when I was twelve years old, working as a stock boy at a local grocer. I've been helping support my family ever since. By fourteen, I was navigating around New York City alone. Each night, I made sure my siblings were fed, bathed, and had homework done. And I was the person who got them to school in the morning. I've helped care for a disabled parent whose moods changed directions like the wind. I've lived a life many thirty-year-olds haven't. And while it might be nice and all to say I should enjoy my innocent youth, I can't go back and reclaim those days. Nor do I want to. I don't regret the choices I've made or even the ones that have been made for me. The years you've been on this Earth physically are pretty damn close to the years I've lived emotionally. Please don't look past me because of my age."

Grasping Corrigan's hands, Sacha shook his head. "I'm not discrediting your experience, but I don't want to hold you back or be the reason your dreams don't come true."

"If they don't, I'll go to Disney World. Besides, dreams are goals without a plan, and I have a plan." He squeezed Sacha's hands. "Look, I know realistically what my odds are to make it into the NHL. I know it's not peaches and cream with travel, practice, and all that jazz. In hockey, you start doing that stuff before you hit varsity if you're serious. Most times, it's the only way to make a varsity team. It's not like football where they wait until you graduate. If that dream doesn't come true for me, it's because it's the wrong dream. And there's nothing that says I can't have more than one." He stepped into Sacha's space. "I don't want to miss out on the dream of us."

Sacha trembled, and his heart pounded against his chest. If there was ever a moment he could feel his blood circulating through him, it was now. He stared at Corrigan knowingly. This man completed him.

Releasing his hands, Sacha trailed his long fingers along Corrigan's jaw and brushed his thumb across his bottom lip. His free hand wrapped around Corrigan's waist, pulled him in, and he tenderly pressed his lips against his younger counterpart. The contact caused Sacha to lose all sense of time and place.

"How dare you!" a voice growled, grounding back in reality.

Sacha peered over Corrigan's shoulder and into the incensed gaze of his father. How long had he been standing there? How had Sacha not heard the door open and close?

He stepped away from Corrigan and straightened his shoulders.

"Yes, I do dare, Father." Reaching across the table, he grabbed his suit jacket draped on the back of the chair. "I don't see a need for a written resignation, but you'll have mine first thing in the morning for your files. That should keep everything nice and neat. By the way, this is my boyfriend. I won't bother with a more formal introduction, as I'm sure you're uninterested and won't be civil."

"You're such a fool."

"I have been, but not as you would think."

"You're throwing away everything important."

"That's where you're wrong. I'm taking the most valuable things in this room—the man I love and my dignity—and I'm leaving." He glanced at Corrigan, whose dark eyes glinted, startled, alarmed, and bewildered simultaneously. "Let's go." Tugging Corrigan's hand, Sacha led him out the door. "I'll have Pax drop my things off to me."

"Sacha!"

"Good day to you, Father," Sacha replied.

Without looking over his shoulder, he exited.

28

CORRIGAN

"I DIDN'T MEAN TO CAUSE PROBLEMS FOR YOU," Corrigan said, waving his arms in the water and staring up at the stars that were beginning to pop out in the sky like scattered diamonds. In the city, he'd never had such an unadulterated view of the evening sky, and he marveled at the beauty before staring across at Sacha, who had his arms draped along the side of the hot tub, his head leaned back, eyes closed, and holding a glass of wine. He looked relaxed—more relaxed than Corrigan had expected.

When the two had parted earlier in the afternoon outside the law center, Corrigan had hesitated to leave. Sacha, despite his even tone, had looked absolutely wrecked yet wholly resolved. He'd explained to Corrigan the situation with his father and, in

Corrigan's opinion, had attempted to pass it off matter-of-factly, as if he wasn't affected. However, Corrigan saw through the facade. He'd wanted to skip his classes and spend the afternoon consoling him, but Sacha wouldn't allow it. Therefore, Corrigan had moved on to Plan B and hightailed it over to Sacha's place the second he was dismissed from hockey practice.

He'd arrived at Sacha's house as Paxton was exiting. "He's out back in the hot tub," Paxton had said, stepping aside for Corrigan to enter. "Fair warning, he's on his third glass of cabernet sauvignon. There's not much reasoning with him."

Corrigan hadn't come prepared for a hot tub rendezvous; therefore, Sacha had offered him a pair of trunks in the pool house, and again, Corrigan's mind was blown. Who kept a stash of new swimwear in varying sizes for guests in their pool house? Then again, if a person had a pool house that resembled a small cottage, it made perfect sense. Even with the copious selection, Corrigan had had difficulty finding a pair that accommodated his thighs and buttocks without too much strain—the quandaries of being a hockey player. After ten minutes of searching, Sacha suggested he go commando. Of course, that had also been Sacha's first suggestion, but Corrigan couldn't help feeling nervous and self-conscious being nude outside where the neighbors could possibly see. It ended up being the option he'd chosen.

"You didn't cause any problems that weren't already there," Sacha answered. "Scabs atop infections don't promote healing."

"But if it wasn't for me, your father—"

"Would still have an issue." Sacha opened his eyes. "His objection isn't with you. It's my entire life, and you happen to be in it. I want you in it." He took a sip of wine and smiled. "And I want you in me."

Corrigan sat up from his reclined position, his eyes wide and brows arched. "You what?"

"Since when did you go deaf?"

"Are you sure?"

"Why wouldn't I be sure?"

Corrigan shook his head. "It's a big decision."

"You don't think I'm a big boy capable of making adult decisions?"

"That's not what I mean." He moved closer to Sacha. "You've been drinking."

"I'm not drunk." He tipped his glass and took a sip. "Yet."

"You're new to this, and it's not a rite of passage

to queerdom. Some gay men never have anal. You've asked yourself, what if you don't like it?"

"What if I do?"

"Sacha—"

"Just because I struggle with a label doesn't mean I don't know what I want, and I'll never know if I don't try. And if I'm going to try, I want to do it with someone who I love and who loves me." He finished his wine and set the glass aside.

Nodding, Corrigan closed the space between them. "I do love you."

"Then I don't see the issue unless you don't want—"

Corrigan interrupted by cupping his hand around the back of Sacha's neck and drawing their mouths together with a kiss that was equally hard, rough, and desperate. There was no way he was going to allow Sacha to finish that sentence when it was not remotely close to being true. He wanted Sacha in a way he'd never wanted anyone. He pushed his tongue inside Sacha's mouth—sucking until they both released hungry growls—while Sacha's hands dug into the curve of Corrigan's lower back and splayed downward.

Pulling away slightly, Corrigan whispered on Sacha's lips, "I want this."

"Then I'll be right back."

———

Sacha

SACHA RETURNED MOMENTS LATER WITH A HANDFUL of condoms and packages of lubricant.

Corrigan chuckled. "Do you think we'll need all that?"

"If I have my way, we will." He placed the items on the shell of the tub, slipped out of his trunks, and slid into the water. "You don't think you're up to it?"

With hockey-quick reflexes, Corrigan snatched Sacha into an embrace and spun him to face away from him. "Overtime is my specialty." Positioning a foot between Sacha's, he pressed against him. His erection blazed against Sacha's inner thigh while his nipples raked tiny sparks of fire across his shoulder blades "I excel in one-on-one shootouts." He allowed his fingers to trail to Sacha's groin and brushed the short pubic hair. "You trimmed."

"You like?"

"Very much," he rasped, nuzzling his neck. "Lean forward."

Sacha complied, resting his arms and upper torso against the cedar decking that encased the hot tub. Corrigan's tone alone caused Sacha's entire body to flitter with uncontrollable anticipation. In the water's reflection, Sacha watched Corrigan retrieve the package of lubricant and squeeze a generous amount in his palms.

"Is that necessary in water?"

"Oddly, yes. You'd be surprised how drying water can be."

Sacha peered over his shoulder. "Sounds like you've done this a time or three."

"Don't be jealous, and no, I haven't. I just happen to be well versed in certain matters."

"And how did that come to be?"

"Oh, for Pete's sake!"

"I don't know Pete."

"A friend—platonic friend," he added quickly, "explained it to me. It's different in a big city, and he didn't want me to get hurt." Corrigan hesitated from rubbing his hands together. "Is that okay?"

"It's not *not* okay with me. At least one of us knows what to do. I just don't like the thought of you being with other men." He paused. "Or women."

"I've never had sex with a woman. I'm what some call a *gold star*." He pressed back against Sacha.

"Haven't you ever been curious?"

"Not really. I told you, I was young when I discovered my attraction to men. It's a heterosexual misnomer that a gay man needs to do a test run with a woman to determine if he's genuinely gay."

"I envy you."

Corrigan softened his voice and placed a series of gentle kisses on Sacha's shoulder. "Sacha, a label isn't everything. You've helped teach me that. Getting caught up on what we call ourselves can cause us to miss out on what's before us. I don't want to miss out on you." He slid his lubricated hands over the curve of Sacha's ass and kneaded his flesh in time with the movement of his mouth on Sacha's shoulder.

Whatever words Sacha intended to vocalize were preempted by the sensation of Corrigan's hands and hypnotizing tongue on his body. "Mm." *Yes.*

Corrigan's finger pressed against Sacha's opening but didn't push in. Instinctively, Sacha clenched.

"Relax," Corrigan whispered, nipping Sacha's earlobe. "I'll go slow. I won't hurt you."

Sacha exhaled, trusting Corrigan but doubting

there would be zero pain involved. "Kiss me while you do it."

Corrigan licked his way from Sacha's ear to his mouth. His kisses were softer but deeper, as if he meant to extract Sacha's soul. In truth, Sacha wasn't certain that wasn't what was happening as he felt himself lifting and floating. Nothing else seemed to matter or exist. However, a sharp pain bolted him back to reality, but only for a moment. Within seconds, the pain eased, and he felt the decadence of Corrigan's fingers rubbing the sensitive nerves inside his hole. Moments later, he felt his muscles relaxing, allowing Corrigan's fingers to glide in and out effortlessly. He moaned again, sounds that probably would have been embarrassing had he not been consumed with pleasure, until Corrigan withdrew to reach for a condom.

This is happening. His breath rushed into his lungs, heating his entire chest. "Don't just have sex with me. Make love to me," he murmured, bracing himself.

"I will." With his hips, Corrigan nudged Sacha's knees farther apart to gain a better position between them. Then, with one silky, slow glide, he entered him.

"Fuck!" Sacha uttered as his vision went black.

His head flexed forward, and he broke out in a gloss of sweat. He wasn't prepared. Corrigan's finger penetration was nothing close to his thickness, and Sacha's knees buckled. A thunderous delectation suffused him.

"You okay?"

Sacha wasn't certain if he answered with words, but he must have given some encouraging indication, because Corrigan continued until he'd filled him.

"Get at me," he purred, clutching the edge of the hot tub for balance. He didn't want Corrigan holding back, although, he had a feeling he might be asking to unleash a kraken that would ravish him into bits and pieces. The practical Sacha would have worried, but the lustful Sacha... not so much.

Nodding, Corrigan began moving with strong and slow thrusts that grew steady, his right hand stroking Sacha's shaft at the same tempo.

I'm going to implode. He pushed back to meet Corrigan's thrust.

"Damn, Sacha," Corrigan panted. "If you keep doing that—"

"Overruled!" Sacha cried, cutting Corrigan's sentence short. Corrigan had hit that magic spot that Sacha had no idea existed. "Again."

Corrigan rammed as deep as he could, and a guttural grunt of agony and delight tumbled from Sacha.

Sacha lost all sense of time and gravity as if he'd been sucked into a vortex. His mind spun, and a coiled tension in his abdomen tightened until it combusted into a million glorious shards of bliss and madness. Again, he wasn't prepared for the violent sweetness that overtook and shook him. Rolling waves of ecstasy gushed through him, and his pulsating cock splattered his release against the side of the tub.

This is what it's supposed to be. Finally, he understood the hoopla regarding sex.

He was still shuddering when Corrigan clutched him in a death grip and stilled. Sacha looked over his shoulder just as Corrigan growled and seemed disoriented with orgasmic rapture.

Beautiful.

For several minutes, neither moved nor spoke and enjoyed the connection of their limp and ravaged bodies. However, Corrigan finally withdrew, breaking their seal. Although Sacha logically knew his body needed a respite, he wanted Corrigan back in him.

"I'm going to assume from the circumstantial

evidence of moaning and groaning that you enjoyed yourself, counselor."

Turning, Sacha wrapped his arms around the neck of the younger man and smiled. "And you'd assume correctly. Seems you know how to handle a stick."

Corrigan winced at the pun. "Extremely corny."

"Do you have to go back to the dorm tonight?"

Corrigan nodded. "Not for a couple hours, though." He sighed. "College hockey life. It'll be like this for the next four years, you know."

"It's a curfew, not a prison sentence. We'll have plenty of time to see each other, just maybe not always as much as we want or when. Where would we be in this world if people gave up every time things got inconvenient?"

"Inconvenient? Don't you mean difficult?"

"Nope. See, that's the issue. People tend to be too egocentric and then write a narrative that life with others is too demanding."

"Relationships are a challenge."

"No they're not, but they are worth being challenged."

"You've lost me."

"I wanted to be an attorney. I studied, took tests. I didn't quit when I failed an exam."

Corrigan quirked an eyebrow and smirked. "*You* failed an exam?"

"Well, no, but that's not the point." He twirled his fingers on Corrigan's nape. "Being an attorney was important to me. Therefore, I did the things I had to do to make that happen, and sometimes that meant missing out on doing things I wanted to do with people equally as important to me or even doing things I didn't like to reach the end goal. Some people viewed that as me putting myself and what I wanted, my ambition, in front of the people in my life and what matters to them. But what would the flipside have been? What if I had done all those other things and flunked out? Would I have been happy? Would my misery have made others happy? Would I even have the capacity to make another happy?"

"I get what you're saying."

"No, I don't believe you do. What does it say about our relationship if we're the type of people who need to be underfoot twenty-four seven to remain connected? Psychopathic codependency? We'd fair better investing in cling wrap. Corrigan, when you love someone, you're there for them, and that doesn't always translate to a physical presence. It's emotional too. All couples face hardships, but they must make a decision to overcome them together. And it's best if they make this decision from the start instead of getting halfway in bumbling about with no plan to love each other every day even when the other doesn't deserve it. I fully comprehend that you're on a journey to be a professional hockey player, and I'm willing to make it with you."

"And I with you."

"Good. Now that that's settled, we should get out of this tub before we do some serious dermatological damage."

29

CORRIGAN

CORRIGAN SNUGGLED BESIDE SACHA, HIS LEGS SLUNG across Sacha's thigh, on the handwoven double-quilted hammock hung between two massive dogwood trees in Sacha's backyard as the golden rays of the setting sun faded. With his head pressed against his companion's chest, Corrigan listened to the older man's heartbeat while his hand stroked down Sacha's side. He sighed, welcoming the breeze that brought with it the sweet scent of juniper.

"Tired?" Sacha asked.

"Hot. How do you deal with this heat? It's like Satan's sweatshop, only it's hot for no damn reason."

"It's the humidity. You'll get used to it."

"Doubtful." Corrigan gazed upward. "But I could get used to chilling in this hammock."

Sacha grunted and pointed at the trees. "You say that now, but stick around for the spring when these towers of kindling unleash their flower baby gravy. Your sinuses will loathe you."

"I guess that means we'll have to cuddle in your bed instead."

"Yep. What a hardship to spend hours upon hours together in my Alaskan king-size bed."

"I definitely could get with that." Closing his eyes, Corrigan smiled. As he began drifting off, a thought suddenly jarred him awake. "Could you get used to somewhere else? Like maybe a northern state?"

"Why would I?"

Corrigan shrugged as if he didn't have an answer but really did. "I don't know," he mumbled. "I was wondering if I got picked up by some team far away...."

"Ah!" Sacha drew it out as if a lightbulb suddenly illuminated above his head. "Then that's where we'll be. Or maybe we'd purchase a condo and live there during the season and keep this place as a vacation home."

"And your career?"

"I can set up practice anywhere." Sacha grinned and added, "Or retire and collect my Social Security."

Corrigan lightly punched him in the shoulder. "Stop that, Grandpa."

"You and I are a team."

Lifting himself to his elbows, Corrigan stared down at Sacha with a huge smile. "We are."

The best team ever, and the future is ours.

THANK YOU SO MUCH FOR READING *FUTURE GOALS*. IF your interest has been piqued and you want to discover more gorgeous hockey players, check out OUT OF THE PENALTY BOX. But why stop there? There are other players to get to know. Check out the entire LOCKER ROOM LOVE series.

ACKNOWLEDGMENTS

The process of writing and having published *Future Goals* has been a long one, and I have so many people to thank and shout-out for helping me along this journey. I must thank my mini who constantly reminded me I needed to be writing instead of watching YouTube and TikTok videos. (Yeah, that really happened.)

A huge thank-you to my alpha and beta readers, cover artist, critique partners, editors, proofers, and publishers for everything, and I do mean everything. I had questions, and y'all gave me the answers. Y'all even gave me answers to questions I didn't know I had, and I'm much appreciative.

Thank you to my family and friends for understanding all the times I bailed on events to research, write, or edit, and checking on me to ensure I'd maintained sanity during computer malfunctions. You each mean the world to me.

Last but certainly not least, I want to thank each

and every person who read, shared, tweeted, blogged, followed, reviewed, or help spread the word about *Future Goals*. It is for you that I write, and that this book is possible. Thank you so very much.

ABOUT THE AUTHOR

Genevive Chamblee is a southern darling and resides in the bayou country where sweet tea and SEC football reign supreme. She is known for being witty (or so she thinks), getting lost anywhere beyond her front yard (the back is pushing it as she's very geographically challenged), falling in love with shelter animals (and she adopts them), asking off-the-beaten-path questions that makes one go "hmm", and preparing home-cooked Creole meals that are as spicy as her writing. Genevive specializes in spinning steamy, romantic tales with humorous flair, diverse characters, and quirky views of love and human behavior. She also is not afraid to delve into darker romances as well.

As an author, I'm very much interested in knowing readers thoughts and feelings. One way that allows me to know is when readers leave reviews. I would appreciate you taking the time to leave a review on your favourite book site (e.g., Amazon or Goodreads). Good, bad, or indifferent, all feedback is welcomed as it helps me grow as a writer and produce the stories readers want to read.

If you would like to keep abreast of news and updates including all new releases, join my mailing list at HTTPS://GENEVIVECHAMBLEECONNECT.WORD PRESS.COM/NEWSLETTER/

I love to hear from you directly, too. Please feel free to email me at genevivechamblee@yahoo.com or check out my website Creole Bayou at WWW. GENEVIVECHAMBLEECONNECT.WORDPRESS.COM for updates.

ABOUT THE PUBLISHER

Hot Tree Publishing loves love. Publishing adult romantic fiction, HTPubs are all about diverse reads featuring heroes and heroines to swoon over. Since opening in 2015, HTPubs have published more than 300 titles across the wide and diverse range of romantic genres. If you're chasing a happily ever after in your favourite subgenre, HTPubs have you covered.

Interested in discovering more amazing reads brought to you by Hot Tree Publishing? Head over to the website for information:

WWW.HOTTREEPUBLISHING.COM

CPSIA information can be obtained
at www.ICGtesting.com
Printed in the USA
BVHW070313310123
657438BV00001B/28

9 781922 679420